The Reluctant Elf

MICHELE GORMAN

Notting Hill Press
PUBLISHINGS THIRD WAY

Copyright © 2014 Michele Gorman

All characters and events in this publication, other than those clearly in the public domain, are fictitious and any resemblance to real persons, living or dead, is purely coincidental.

All rights reserved. No part of this publication may be reproduced, stored in a retrieval system, or transmitted, in any form or by any means, without the prior permission of the publisher

ISBN: 150273625X
ISBN-13: 978-1502736253

ALSO BY MICHELE GORMAN

Perfect Girl
The Curvy Girls Club
Christmas Carol
Bella Summer Takes a Chance
Single in the City (The Expat Diaries: I)
Misfortune Cookie (The Expat Diaries: II)
Twelve Days to Christmas (The Expat Diaries: III)

This novella is dedicated to Kate Crisp, who generously took part in CLIC Sargent's charity auction to have a character named for her. Hope you love Aunt Kate!

CLIC Sargent is the UK's leading cancer charity for children and young people, and their families. They provide clinical, practical, financial and emotional support to help them cope with cancer and get the most out of life. They are there from diagnosis onwards and aim to help the whole family deal with the impact of cancer and its treatment, life after treatment and, in some cases, bereavement.

http://www.clicsargent.org.uk

CHAPTER ONE

I know I'm dreaming by the way the gorgeous young man holds my hand and gazes into my eyes. A real man hasn't looked at me with such devotion since the time I reprogrammed my friend's husband's PlayStation.

Just as the dream man leads me from the pub table into his bedroom next door – what the hell, it's my dream, right? – and I start wondering if I've dream-shaved my legs, his mobile begins to ring.

'Are you going to get that?'

'Get what?' he murmurs into my hair. 'I don't hear anything.'

'Your phone is ringing.'

Aggravation starts nibbling at my ardor as the ringing grows louder.

'I don't hear it.'

'Oh, for God's sake.' I can't even get any peace and quiet in my own imagination.

But there is no dream man and his phone isn't ringing.

My landline is.

I glance at the bedside alarm clock. 1.36am. The hour of emergencies and booty calls. My booty hadn't been called since Tony Blair was Prime Minister, so my quickening pulse is panic, not passion.

'Hello?' My voice comes out oatmeal-thick.

'Is this Lottie Crisp?'

'Yes.' The panic intensifies. Mabel. Is it Mabel? No. She's sound asleep in the other room. At least I think she is.

'This is Doctor Londergan at Glan Clwyd hospital in Bodelwyddan.'

As the woman continues talking I run with the phone to my daughter's door and push it open. Her little body hardly makes a bump under her Spiderman duvet. One socked foot sticks out over the edge. Unlike me, Mabel has no fear of monsters under the bed or anywhere else. I could learn a thing or two from my seven-year-old.

Of course I want to pounce on her, but sleeping dogs and children are best left undisturbed.

'I'm afraid there's been an accident involving your Aunt Kate,' Doctor Londergan says. 'Her car went off the road the day before yesterday. We've been trying to reach her family and just now got your details.'

'I'm her only family.' The rushing in my ears threatens to drown out her voice. 'Is she dead?'

'No, she's alive, in Intensive Care. Can you come?'

'Not until morning. The next train to Wales won't be until morning.'

'Come as soon as you can,' she says. 'We've induced a coma to help her body recover.'

This can't be happening again.

Aunt Kate is the liveliest person I've ever known. Though I'd have said that about my parents too and look how they ended up.

It's still dark when I creep into Mabel's room early the next morning.

'Sugarpea?' I rub her duvet-warm back and listen for her breathing to change. 'Mabel? Wake up.'

She inhales one long breath and exhales her objection. 'Not yet, Mummy.'

'I'm sorry, we have to get up extra-early this morning. We get to go to Wales today.' I shudder to think about everything that won't get done now before we leave.

At least Celine packed Mabel's bag before she flew to the Philippines for her own Christmas holiday. She knew I'd most likely bring Mabel to Wales with fifteen jumpers, her favorite blue tutu and no socks. Without Celine watching over us, we'd be on first name terms with social services by now.

'But we don't leave for two days,' says Mabel, rubbing her eyes with the back of her hand.

'We have to go early.'

She sits up. 'I can't, Mummy. I have other plans.'

'I know Theresa's birthday is tomorrow but this is important.' She's been looking forward to her best friend's party for nearly a month. 'You can still ring her to wish her happy birthday.'

My daughter's jaw sets. Whenever she does that I see her father.

It's the only time I ever see him.

'Please, Mabel, don't make this difficult. Now get up and brush your teeth. We have to leave in twenty minutes to make our train.'

'I'm not going!' She throws the duvet over her head. 'I told you I have other plans.'

'You are going, young lady, so get up and brush your teeth. I'll pack us some breakfast for the train. Come on. Now!'

'You're a terrible Mummy!' she cries. 'And I hope that one day a big hairy monster comes and flushes you down the loo.'

I can't smile. I'll lose this battle if I do. That's lesson number one in controlling a child. I just wish I knew what lesson number two through infinity are.

'Well, until I'm flushed away you're stuck with me.' I yank the duvet down and kiss her soft blonde hair. 'Teeth brushed please, and I'll explain everything when we're on the train.

I need some time to find a way to explain that what I told her three years ago might be a lie.

We board the 7.15 to Rhyl at Euston Station with just a few other passengers. It's still four days before Christmas and most people will have to work tomorrow to wrap up before they go off for the holidays.

I've emailed my boss to tell him I'm leaving early. As a software developer he's best communicated with in binary code but I didn't have time to write a program that said Sorry-I'm-leaving-my-project-unfinished-but-my-family-is-more-important-than-the-latest-war-game-for-children. Maybe animated with a dancing paperclip. It won't be the first time we've missed a deadline, or the first time I've disappointed him. Luckily he's a patient man.

Mabel is in a slightly better mood by the time we find our seats. 'I can't wait to see Aunt Kate!' she says. 'Do you think she'll have Welsh cakes for us when we arrive? I could just *murder* a Welsh cake.'

That child sponges up everything I say. Mimicry is supposed to be the sincerest form of flattery but it's not. It's the surest form of reproach when it makes your seven-year-old sound like she's twenty-seven.

I remind myself, again, to watch what I say in front of her.

'We're going early because we need to see Aunt Kate in the hospital.'

'Is she there getting her nose refreshed?'

When I went with my friend for moral support to her nose job surgery last year, I told Mabel she was going in to freshen up her nose.

'No, Aunt Kate's nose is just fine the way it is.' I hope that's still true. 'She's in the hospital because she's had an accident.'

'Not in that house I hope? It's a death trap.'

I cringe at my words parroted back at me. 'No, in a car.'

Her eyes widen. 'Like Granny and Granddad?' she whispers. 'You said it wouldn't happen again.'

'No, no! Not like them. The doctor said that Aunt Kate is still-' Alive, I almost say. 'She's in the hospital and the doctors are doing everything they can to make her better so she can spend Christmas with us.'

Mabel slumps against me. 'I was scared. I'm glad she's all right.'

Then she straightens up. 'Can I give her my Christmas present early? That might cheer her up.'

Finally, the tears come and I look out the window so

Mabel won't see them. I'm not sure I can go through this again.

It had been early morning when the doctor called from the A&E in Australia. That made it late evening there, but the doctor hadn't had to search for my contact details that time. Mum and Dad had everything neatly written in a small notebook in Mum's handbag. They were careful people like that.

'Is this Lottie Crisp?'

As soon as I heard the man's bouncy accent I knew something was wrong.

It was my parents' dream holiday to spend a month touring around Australia. I knew their itinerary off by heart. A week in Sydney, then a flight to Melbourne where they'd visit some friends, then a two-week drive through the outback.

'Miss Crisp,' said the man as I braced myself. His laid back accent didn't fool me. 'There's been an accident involving your parents. I'm terribly sorry.'

I only half-heard the rest of what he said. The outback, drunk driver, Mum killed instantly and Dad dead on arrival at the hospital. Could I come?

I had to bring their bodies back to England. That was the worst part of the first few days, travelling on that plane knowing my parents were lying in the hold with all the holidaymakers' luggage.

Aunt Kate came to stay with Mabel so that I could go. We'd had just a few hours together before I had to leave for Heathrow. Despite the fact that it was her only brother who'd died, and her beloved sister-in-law, she was as rock-solid as the Welsh cakes she made for Mabel's tea.

'I would do anything to take this pain away, my sweet Lottie, anything,' she said as she pulled me to her ample bosom with the grip of a Sumo wrestler. 'I'm here for you, do you understand? Whatever you need, I'm here for you, my darling girl. We'll get through this together, you, me and Mabel.'

We did get through it, together, though I've had more than a few harsh words since then for whoever decides our fates.

If they now think they're going to take my Aunt Kate too, they've got another thing coming. We Crisps are tough as old boots.

CHAPTER TWO

Our journey to Rhyl is smooth but my mind skitters from one horrific scenario to another. What will I find when we get to the hospital? If only I could rewind the past seventy-two hours and keep Aunt Kate safely off the road. She's got the eyesight of a disorientated mole and should never have been driving anyway. Had everything gone to plan, Mabel and I would be arriving in two days' time, ready to enjoy our first Welsh countryside Christmas with Aunt Kate at her B&B.

She's run the business since before Mabel was born but always shuts up between Christmas and New Year's so she can travel to London to stay with us.

This year though, Aunt Kate has to take in paying guests for the holidays. It's the last thing she wants to do but there's the small matter of her bank manager to consider. It's always hard to pin Aunt Kate down on details but something about her loan being dependent on the B&B getting a certain rating by the end of the year means that she has to host the reviewer over

Christmas. So Mabel and I said we'd bring the Crisp family Christmas to her instead.

That was the idea anyway.

My mood matches the weather by the time the train pulls into Rhyl station. We're the only passengers to exit the two-carriage train and through the slanting rain I can see that it's a typical out-of-season Victorian resort town. Ornate ironwork, with its paintwork tattooed with rust from the sea air, supports a glass roof. Come summer the beachfront probably bustles with swim-suited families, burnt to a crisp and ready to eat their own weight in Welsh rock and candy floss.

I tuck Mabel's scarf into her collar and pull my coat more tightly around me.

'This is where Aunt Kate lives?' she asks.

'No, I think she's about fifteen miles from here in an area called Snowdonia.'

'Will there be snow there?'

'It feels cold enough but I don't think so, not where the B&B is anyway. Maybe up in the mountains.'

'Are we going there now?'

'Not yet. We need to go see her at the hospital first, remember?'

A lone car sits with its taxi light on at the front of the station.

The driver gets out to load our bags in the boot.

'We're going to Glan Clyde hospital, please.'

'Glan Clue-Id,' he says, pulling his huge sheepskin coat more tightly around his tall frame. He's disheveled in a way that would shout "hipster" in London, but something about his stained jeans and ancient boots tells me that his stubble and too-long dark hair aren't meant to be fashion statements.

'Yes, the A&E department, please.'

He pulls out from the station like he's fleeing the scene. We bomb up the quiet road and careen around the corner.

'You can slow down a little. It's not an emergency.'

I turn to Mabel. 'Here, check that your seatbelt is on tightly.'

But his motoring skills don't improve as we hurtle along the rural two-lane road, sandwiched between the sea and sheep-filled fields. If this is the standard of road safety around here I'm not surprised Aunt Kate crashed her car.

My heart races when the hospital comes into view fifteen minutes later. What if we get to the desk and the nurse looks at us with pity as she works out how to tell us that we're too late?

No, I won't think like that. For Mabel's sake I have to stay positive, even if my insides are liquefying with fear.

'We're here to see Kate Crisp, please,' I tell the plump, pleasant-looking woman at the reception desk. 'She's in Intensive Care.'

This feels like a shameful admission.

She taps her keyboard. 'Just down that corridor, love. Now what you do is go through the double doors on your left. The nurse inside can take you straight to her.'

'Oh, okay, that's brilliant, thank you!' I find myself smiling. She's got the type of positive bedside manner that could make you look forward to having your leg amputated.

When we get to the Intensive Care desk the young nurse says, 'You're looking for Ms. Crisp? She's right this way.' As if we're just meeting her for lunch.

We follow her down another short corridor.

'Please clean your hands whenever you go into the room.'

I gesture for Mabel to hold her palms under the liquid disinfectant.

'It stinks.'

'I know it does, but it kills the germs.'

'Does it smother them?'

'Something like that.'

Aunt Kate has the room to herself. She's in the bed closest to the door, with a mask over her face and tubes running from her arms.

'Is she dead?' Mabel whispers.

I shake my head, not trusting my voice. Her face is swollen and her forehead has turned a nasty shade of purple. There's a stitched-up laceration over her eye. 'She's just sleeping.'

'I'll see if the doctor is free,' the nurse says, hurrying out.

I go to my aunt and gently touch her hand. 'I'm here, Aunt Kate. Mabel and I are here.'

'Can she hear you?'

'I'm not sure, but I think so. Do you want to talk to her? I'm sure she'd love to hear you.'

She nods and shuffles very close to the bed.

'Hi Aunt Kate, it's me, Mabel. You'll probably know it's me even with your eyes closed because of my voice. We had a nice journey on the train. We had regular seats but then because there weren't many people on, we moved to a table. Mummy said it was better for her computer but then she forgot her computer and she swore. Not the F word, though, just the S word. I still told her that ladies don't swear. That's right, isn't it Mummy?'

'That's right, I shouldn't have said that.'

A fifty-something woman joins us as Mabel continues to talk to Aunt Kate as though they're chatting over tea and cake.

Doctor Londergan smiles as she introduces herself. She takes Aunt Kate's chart from the end of the bed and then gestures outside.

'I'll just be out here, Mabel. I bet Aunt Kate would love to hear about your Christmas pageant.'

'She's in a coma?' I ask Doctor Londergan under the bright corridor lights.

'Yes, a medically induced coma. There's a lot of swelling around her brain so we want to help it heal by eliminating any non-essential functions.'

'So it's not a coma like the ones where you don't know if she's going to wake up?'

Doctor Londergan shakes her head. 'We've administered drugs to induce it, so once we remove the drugs, she'll wake up.'

'When will you do that?'

'Not until the swelling has gone down in her brain. There may not be brain damage but we won't know for sure until the swelling subsides. That could take a few days or a few weeks. We're monitoring her closely and, as you can see, she's on a respirator to help her breathe.'

'So she's going to be okay?'

'She was very lucky she was wearing her seatbelt. As was the other passenger, but the other car impacted on your Aunt's side, which is why she sustained more serious injuries. She's also got a broken tibia – her leg –

which we've set. That should heal within six to eight weeks and then she can have the cast removed. Do you have any more questions?'

'No. Yes. You said there was a passenger? Who was it?'

She glances at her paperwork. 'A Ms. Evans was also involved in the accident.'

Ms. Evans? I think she's Aunt Kate's cook, though she usually called her by her job description. 'And she's all right?'

'She fractured her arm but she was treated and discharged. I believe she's staying with her niece over in Dyserth. Do you know it?'

'No, I'm not from around here.' As if that isn't obvious from my London accent. 'Do you have her phone number?'

'I'll have the nurse get it for you when you leave. The visiting hours in Intensive Care are from five o'clock till seven each evening. You can stay today because you've just arrived and there's no one else in with your aunt. Will you be coming back tomorrow?'

Yes, I tell her, and every day until Aunt Kate is well again. There's no way I'll leave her. Mabel and I will be spending Christmas in Wales.

'Please leave your contact details with reception,' says Doctor Londergan. 'And will you be staying at her house?'

'Yes. We'll be there if you need us. Oh. I haven't got keys.'

'Everything she had in the car is in the cabinet by her bed. If her keys are there, feel free to take them with you.'

'Thank you. Can I go back in to her now?'

'Of course. I'm sorry this happened so close to Christmas,' she says from the doorway. 'This probably isn't how you thought you'd be spending the holiday.'

Definitely not. Then I remember why Aunt Kate couldn't come to London this year.

The reviewer and his family don't know about the accident. They'll still arrive on the 24th expecting a Christmas holiday.

I lean down to kiss Aunt Kate's cool cheek.

'You don't have to worry about anything, Aunt Kate, just concentrate on getting well. I'll take good care of the B&B until you're fit again, I promise.'

When the reception nurse gives me the phone number where Cook is staying I ring it straightaway. I'm going to need a lot of help over the coming week.

'Hello, is that Ms. Evans?'

'No, it's her niece Bronwyn. Who's this?'

I remember that Bronwyn is Aunt Kate's cleaner. Perfect. I'll need her help too. She listens as I explain who I am.

'What do you want?'

She sounds angry. Surely she isn't blaming me or Aunt Kate for what happened?

'Well, I wondered when your aunt will be able to come back to work.'

'Probably in the new year,' she says.

'The new year! But we need her now! I understand that she's recovering from the accident, and maybe she can't cook easily with a broken arm, but I was hoping…'

'It's impossible. We're leaving tomorrow morning,' she says. 'We're going to Spain to recuperate.'

'What, both of you? But you're the housekeeper and

you weren't even in the accident. Aren't you coming to work either?'

'No, as I said, we're going to Spain. You can't expect me to send my poorly auntie on her own.'

'But who's going to clean the B&B while you're gone?'

'I didn't know I'd be needed, did I? With Kate in hospital, I didn't think there'd be any work for me anyway. I've got to go. Auntie is waiting for her lunch.'

'Wait, please, wait,' you skiving little cow, I don't say. 'If your aunt can't come to work, could she at least tell me what I need to know about the place? I've never even been there.'

'She's not up to talking right now.'

'Could she, I don't know, email me or fax the B&B or something with some instructions? Here's my email address.'

I'm not convinced she's writing anything down.

'Please. I have no idea what I'm doing. Can you please ask her to at least do that before you leave?'

She sighs. 'I'll ask her, but we're very busy. We have to pack and EasyJet charges a fortune for checked bags. I don't know how we're going to get everything into carry-ons.'

I'll take their luggage concerns over singlehandedly hosting a critic and his family any day.

It's still raining when we leave the hospital. I should have asked reception to call us a taxi.

'Here, button up, Mabel, so you don't catch a cold.'

A car pulls up and the door opens.

'You again?' I say to the taxi driver who dropped us off.

'I waited.'

'We went in over an hour ago. You didn't need to wait.'

'You're probably my only fare for the day,' he says. 'Are you going back to the train station?'

'No, to my Aunt's B&B.'

I read him the address from the letter Aunt Kate sent with directions for our arrival.

Again he corrects my pronunciation.

'Mummy, we're staying at Aunt Kate's when she's not there?'

'Yes, because we'll want to see her every day until she's well, won't we? And we can make the house look lovely for when she comes home.'

We don't have any alternative. In three days a houseful of guests will arrive. Someone has to be there to welcome them or Aunt Kate won't have a business to come home to.

Granted, I'm not the most domesticated of goddesses, but I'll do my best. The B&B should impress the reviewer on looks alone. Even though I've never seen it, thanks to Aunt Kate's descriptions over the years I can picture it as clearly as if I lived there. Its grand two story Victorian façade, formal parlor and library, large hall and dining room will be the perfect backdrop for Christmas. There'll be cozy evenings playing board games in front of the roaring fire or snuggled up with a book on one of the embroidered sofas. If the sun shines during the day then the guests can relax in the conservatory that looks out to the hills. It sounds like heaven. The rating will just be a formality, really.

Besides, it's not like I have any idea how to get in

touch with the guests to explain what's happened anyway.

Like it or not, I'm about to become a B&B hostess.

CHAPTER THREE

I have to tell the taxi driver again to slow down. He seems to have little working knowledge of his brake pedal and keeps swerving over the center line. But after thirty fraught minutes, we turn into a steep drive.

'Are you sure this is the address? It doesn't look right.'

The winter-bare trees have shed many of their branches, which the taxi's wheels crunch over as we pull into the circular drive. And the house is, well…

He takes Aunt Kate's letter from me again.

'Yes, this is it. I'll get your bags.'

I know I should get out and help him, but I'm rooted to the back seat.

The house is completely derelict. The once-white stucco and mock-Tudor façade is streaked and stained with neglect. The elements have bowed and bloated the window sills.

Speaking of the elements, the attic is exposed to them. One corner of the steeply gabled roof is tile-free.

The wooden joists poke out like badly broken bones.

I just can't reconcile what I'm seeing with Aunt Kate's descriptions of her dreamy gingerbread house in the woods. This isn't a dream house. It's a nightmare.

'This place is a dump!'

I begin to sob as the enormity of what I've promised Aunt Kate sinks in. That reviewer and his whole family will arrive, *to this*, in less than seventy-two hours.

'Mummy, is it haunted?'

Mabel, usually the first one to want to explore, holds my hand tightly.

It's certainly haunted by the ghosts of Aunt Kate's failed dreams. How could I have let her live in a place like this for all these years? I should have come up long before this.

'I'm sure it's not haunted, sugarpea. After all, it's Aunt Kate's home.'

'Then why are you crying?'

'Oh, I'm being silly. It's just that there's a lot to do before Aunt Kate's guests arrive.'

The driver opens my door. 'Is everything all right?'

His deep brown eyes are full of concern. Or maybe he thinks I can't pay his fare.

My legs shake as I stand up. 'Not really, no. In fact it's about as far from all right as I can imagine. We've got paying guests coming for Christmas in three days and the cook and housekeeper are buggering off to Spain. I'm all alone here.'

'Oh, well, Bronwyn has always wanted to go to the Costa del Sol.'

'Well I'm glad she'll finally get to work on her tan, but where does that leave me? I can't run this whole place by myself. I have no idea what I'm doing. And look at it.'

Tears fill my eyes again. It's hopeless. I can't even cook.

The look of pity on the driver's kind face gives me an idea.

'Can *you* cook?' I ask.

His expression turns from pity to suspicion. 'Why?'

'Because if you can, I'll give you £1,000 cash to help me for the next few days. Until the 26th when the guests leave.'

'Well I can't really-'

'Please! I don't know what else to do. My aunt is in a coma. That's why we were at the hospital. And it's too late now to cancel the guests' stay. Not that I'd even know how to get in touch with them. So they're coming, and it's a reviewer and his family. Aunt Kate scheduled them because she needs a star rating or the bank will force her to sell the B&B. This is her whole life. Do you know my aunt?'

He shakes his head, rubbing the dark stubble that peppers his chin. 'I only know Bronwyn because we were at school together. A thousand quid you said? Cash?'

'Yes, and I'll even give you half today and half on the 26th. I'd need you to cook and help me get the place fixed up before they come. Well, basically I'll need you to do whatever you can to help. Is it a deal?'

I pray he'll say yes. Otherwise Mabel is going to have to pick up some carpentry skills pretty quickly.

He puts his hand out and envelops mine in its warmth. 'Deal. I'll drive you to the cash machine back in Rhyl. I'm Danny. What's your name?'

'Lottie, and this is Mabel. Nice to meet you.'

I just hope he's more domestic than I am.

This is probably going to sound impossibly spoiled and sheltered, but I only lived away from my parents for a few years when I went to university. That's where I fell in love with Mabel's father and, full of excitement and the folly of youth, played fast and loose with the birth control.

I knew almost as soon as I saw those two pink lines on the wee stick that I wanted the little person growing inside me, and that my parents would be supportive. I never imagined just what a support they'd become.

I waddled through my final year's classes, morning-, noon- and night-sick but so excited to meet my child at the end of the term. She came into the world with a full head of hair and a strong set of lungs and we've been a family of two ever since.

I moved back to my parents' Hampstead house where my old room was waiting for me. Mum painted the spare room lilac and stenciled fairies all over the walls for her granddaughter.

By then Celine had been part of our family for nearly my whole life. We didn't have much extra money when I was growing up but with both Mum and Dad working at the university, they needed someone to look after the house and, sometimes, me. Celine started as a one-day-a-week cleaner but she soon worked her way into my parents' hearts and stomachs. She always found time to cook delicious dinners on the days she came. Eventually the whole family was addicted to her Filipino dishes and she stayed with us every day.

When I was around ten her landlord tried extorting her for more rent. Falsely believing she didn't have a work permit, he threatened to report her to Immigration if she didn't pay up. That was when Dad invited Celine to live with us. Her salary remained the same but she'd never have to worry about her living situation again. As long as the house in Hampstead was in our family, Celine had a home.

With such a fantastic cook in the house it's no wonder I never really learned my way around the kitchen. Perhaps if I'd lived with Mabel's father things might have been different, but that was never going to happen.

Mabel, Danny the driver and I arrive back at the B&B, me with a lighter bank account and Danny with a grin on his face.

The house's prospects haven't improved in our absence. If anything they look even more dire.

'Time to go inside,' I say to Mabel, taking the hand she offers me. A tiny part of me hopes that we'll be surprised. Maybe Aunt Kate concentrated her efforts inside where her guests spent the most time. Then who'd care if the outside was a bit shabby?

Aunt Kate used to be an opera singer, so maybe she's draped the rooms in sumptuous velvets and brocades. She always had an eye for lovely furniture, and dragged me through Notting Hill and Grays antique market nearly every weekend that she visited. We searched for chairs or tables with elegant legs (Aunt Kate has a thing for elegant legs), brocade footstools and gilded mirrors. All those purchases over the years must have found their way into the B&B.

By the time I wriggle the key in just the right way to open the large wooden front door, I'm nearly sure it'll look like the prop room at the Royal Opera House.

I take about two steps inside the dim hall. 'Oof. Shit!'

'Mummy, are you okay?'

I don't know which to rub first, my throbbing toe or my knees where they've hit the floor. 'I'm fine, I just tripped.' Motherhood is full of small lies.

'You said a swear word.'

'Yes, that wasn't very clever of me, was it?'

'I guess your Aunt planned some renovations,' Danny says. When he sheds his giant coat I can see that he's a bit older than he first seemed, and a few years older than me, probably in his early thirties. 'There must be fifty tins of paint here.'

Exactly why they should be in the middle of the front hall is another matter. As I look around, my hopeful bubble bursts. This is no Royal Opera House.

Three tall windows run along one side of the wide hall and a staircase climbs up the other side. But the grimy window panes let in only weak light.

'We may as well try to see what we're dealing with.'

I hoist up the sash panes on every window so the daylight can reach the darkened corners.

'It's yucky,' Mabel says.

It's worse than yucky. The walls are pockmarked with holes and painted a dreary yellowish brown.

'Who'd use that color in a house?' I ask.

'I think it was probably a different color to start with,' Danny says. 'It's yellowed over the years.'

It's got the patina of nicotine-stained fingers and the far corner is streaked with water damage. The varnish is worn off the floorboards where feet have trod over the decades, and everything needs a good wash. Whatever

Bronwyn does with her time here clearly doesn't involve soap and water.

Slowly we walk through the rest of the house like fearful tomb raiders. Every gasp from Danny or Mabel makes me jump, expecting the worst. It's obvious that the house was once grand. Probably before the First World War. The sitting room is large, overcrowded with Aunt Kate's elegant-legged tables. I run my hand over a small mahogany side table.

'Mabel, do you remember when we found this, in that skip in Highgate?'

She smiles. 'You climbed in with the rubbish.'

The things I do for my Aunt. 'And we brought it home and Dad stripped it?'

Mabel's smile fades. 'Mummy? Will Aunt Kate die like Granny and Granddad did?'

'Ahem, I'll have a look upstairs,' Danny says, considerately absenting himself.

I lead Mabel to one of the silver and red Chinese silk sofas.

'Honey, the doctor said that Aunt Kate should be okay when she wakes up. She's only sleeping now so that her body can heal itself.'

'So she definitely won't die?' Mabel's eyes search my face. I wish I could give her such absolute certainty.

'I don't think she will. I'm not planning on it, that's for sure. Do you still worry about something happening to me?'

When she nods my heart breaks a little. How am I supposed to make her feel secure? I don't have the authority to tell The Grim Reaper to bugger off and bother someone else.

I hug her little body to mine. 'Well I'm not going

anywhere and neither are you. We've got too much living to do!'

She returns my smile.

'Let's go see what the rest of the house looks like, okay?'

'Yes, that's quite enough of this morbid talk for one day,' says my world-weary seven-year-old.

Danny bounds down the stairs just as we come out of the dining room. 'What's the prognosis down here?' he asks.

'It looks like the ceiling is coming down in the dining room and there are mouse droppings in the kitchen sink. How's it looking upstairs?'

He shakes his head. 'Mushrooms are literally growing on the floorboards in the bedrooms, and mold up most of the walls.'

'Maybe you could cook them.'

'Not unless you want to risk poisoning. I think your Aunt was optimistic when she got all that paint. This place needs more than a coat on the walls. It needs a structural engineer.'

Nobody has ever accused Aunt Kate of pessimism.

'Well we've only got three days to do what we can and hope the place doesn't fall down before the guests leave. At least the furniture is all right. There's just too much of it. But yes, Aunt Kate is definitely an optimist.'

While Dad went to university, studied hard and gained respectability in professorial circles, his little sister was traveling by campervan across Europe trying to make a go of her musical career. Whenever their parents told her she was nuts she just laughed and hugged them. There wasn't much that Aunt Kate couldn't overcome with a giggle, a hug, a wing and a prayer.

She did achieve some success as an opera singer, and performed small parts in most of Europe's capitals.

She was never great with money though, and often accepted payment for her roles in clothes instead of cash. After ten years she came back to England with trunks full of gowns and little else. But she didn't mind that. 'My life is rich,' she said. 'My bank account doesn't need to be.'

CHAPTER FOUR

'What are you doing?' Danny asks the next morning, possibly wondering why I'm standing on the dining room table in my pajamas holding my phone towards the crumbling ceiling.

'Oh,' I say, pulling my robe around me. 'You're early.'

It was nearly midnight by the time he left last night. We'd worked straight through but when I got up this morning it didn't look like we'd made much difference.

We did find all the sheets and towels at least, and Aunt Kate's hoarding tendency means there's plenty of formal china and glassware for the guests. Today the heavy work really begins.

'I'm trying to get a signal. I'll try outside in a minute but I wanted to see what the reception was like in the house. So far it's a 3g black hole in here.'

The reviewer may not appreciate having to stand on the dining table to send a text.

'These old walls might look ready to cave in but

they're probably quite thick,' he says. 'You could try the conservatory.'

Sure enough, my phone whistles with new emails when I reach the ornate glasshouse.

The noise excites one of the pigeons making camp on the floor. He takes flight through a broken window while the rest of his cooing friends watch me have a minor heart attack.

'Hey Danny?' I call back inside. 'How are your pigeon-whispering skills? We have feathered houseguests. If you can convince them to go outside we can try to clean all the poo off the floor.'

It's frigid out here but with the wood-burning stove going in the middle of the room and the addition of some sofas and chairs, it might pass for shabby chic instead of just shabby. At least there's a phone signal.

I scroll through my emails, clicking open the one from my boss. *Sorry to hear about your aunt, it reads, and of course I understand that you need to go. Just keep me updated and let me know when you think you'll be back. I hope your aunt is okay.*

I delete the usual proposals from dying African princes to make me their sole heir and click on Bronwyn's email.

It's only a few lines long, but at least it's something.

Dear Lottie, We're at the airport and Bronwyn is typing this on her phone. I'm terribly sorry about your aunt and I do hope she'll be well again soon. Our prayers are with her.

Here's what you need to know about the house:

- Mingus's food is under the sink. He prefers the fish to the chicken but he'll eat whatever you put out when he gets hungry

- Always wait five minutes after flushing the loo to turn on the taps

- There's coal in the cellar for the wood burners
- I believe the reviewer is called Rupert Grey-Smythe
- We have mice
- Watch out for the 8.30 train
- Don't forget about the chickens
Good luck!

We've got chickens? I suppose that means Danny has a fresh supply of eggs to cook. The morning is looking up.

I leave him in the kitchen to acquaint himself with the appliances while I check on Mabel.

'Mummy?' she calls as soon as I open the door.

'Yes, sweetie. Did you sleep well?'

'I'm still sleepy,' she says. 'But I'm too excited to stay in bed.'

'Maybe a shower will wake you up. I'll go in first just to make sure it's working, okay?' I tuck the thick duvet around her. 'Have another little rest and I'll let you know when it's ready.'

There are three bathrooms upstairs to accommodate the seven guest bedrooms but, as Danny pointed out, not all of those rooms are habitable. Actually, depending on your definition of habitable, it's questionable whether any of them are. They all have mold creeping up the walls. A fungal pelt covers the floor in two of them and part of the ceiling is caved in in another. That leaves four guest rooms. I just hope the reviewer won't ask to see the others.

Aunt Kate has clearly done a few renovations in the bathrooms though. They're wet rooms in fact, fully tiled across their floors and halfway up the walls, with a round drain in the middle of the slightly sloping floor.

But they still have all their pre-war features, which makes them so old that they've come all the way around to retro.

There's a cistern above the toilet and a claw-footed tub. The only concession to the latter half of the 20th Century is the hand-held shower nozzle mounted on the wall.

I run the hot water tap, waiting for it to heat. So far so good. Gratefully I peel off my pajamas and set my shampoo in the little tray at the far end of the tub. The round rail suspended above me is bare so I have to be extra careful not to splash. In fact I'll see if Danny can find a plain curtain. Even though the door is locked I feel exposed without it.

The shampoo lathers my hair into stiff peaks. The water must be softer here than in London. Maybe it's well water. Lovely, clean Welsh well water. That could be a selling point to the guests, I suppose-

Suddenly the wall behind the bath moans with the anguish of the undead. Then something starts knocking on the wall, slowly at first, getting faster and faster and faster until….

'Jesus!'

The water scalds me before I can jump away. Shampoo bubbles slide into my eyes as I feel for the edge of the tub.

Ow ow ow ow.

Then there's a crash. Squinting through the bubbles, I see the showerhead writhing on the floor beside the tub, soaking everything.

With my eyes streaming from the soap, I screw the tap handles closed.

'Holy shit.'

'Mummy?' Mabel calls through the bathroom door. 'Can I have my shower now? I've used the loo already.'

Yes, I gathered that from the sudden change in water temperature. Our plumbing is going to poach our guests if we let them shower.

'Hang on honey, I'll draw you a bath instead.'

Mabel has found Mingus, which turns out to be a rather rough-looking cat. He was asleep in the dining room cabinet where Aunt Kate keeps the white linen tablecloths (now covered in brown and black fur). Mabel has decided that Mingus loves her, based on the fact that he'll purr if she strokes him long enough. He seems perfectly happy in his role as her new best friend and I'm glad she's got the diversion. It isn't easy always being the only little person in a grown up world.

I throw the tablecloths into the industrial tumble dryer in the cellar. Hopefully most of the hair will come out in the filter. If not we'll have to convince the guests that mohair tablecloths are the newest mealtime accessory in Snowdonia.

I'm not fooling myself. I know we'll never clean/arrange/paint/fix in time. We've got to prioritize. Aunt Kate must have planned to get the rooms painted, so I send Danny to the guest bedrooms to see what he can do.

Meanwhile I make a start on the downstairs hall, which looks even worse now that the newly cleaned windows let in all the daylight. In some places the walls are so pockmarked that they look like the scene of an execution. Painting over them will just give us freshly painted pockmarked walls.

Aunt Kate, what could you have been thinking,

booking the reviewer in for Christmas? Did you really believe you'd get everything done in time for him to give you the rating you need?

Even as I ask myself the question I know the answer. Of course she did. She believes she can do anything.

This is, after all, the woman who opened a home for retired opera singers in northern Wales.

In fairness, it was her friend Ivan's idea and, at first, his investment.

They were friends from their touring days in Europe in the seventies, and there was nothing she wouldn't do for Ivan. When he retired, at the ripe age of fifty, he was determined to give something back to the art that had given him so much.

Aunt Kate had always been a wandering soul, so why not move to Wales? They used some of his family money to buy the house and offered a home to ageing singers for nearly ten years. It was rare for a tenant to be able to pay them anything, but for a while they were able to make ends meet using Ivan's remaining savings and then an equity release loan against the property.

The money ran out at nearly the same time that Ivan's luck did. Aunt Kate nursed him through his final curtain call and he left all he had to her – the house, the land and the unpaid equity release loan.

That's why I'm sitting in a crumbling house contemplating the holes in the walls.

I can hear Danny saying something from upstairs.

'Be right up.'

When I push the bedroom door open it slams shut in my face.

'Don't come in!'

'Sorry. Are you painting the door?'

'Err, yes? Oh bugger.'

'Danny, what's going on? I'm coming in.'

It looks like the world's largest seagull has taken aim at Danny. 'Spilled a bit of paint, did you?'

'A bit. Sorry. I'll try to be more careful.'

'Just see if you can get some on the walls, okay?'

'I'm not exactly a painting pro,' he says. 'Which is ironic since I went to art school.'

'Did you really?'

'You don't have to sound so incredulous. Yes, I did, really.'

'I'm sorry.' I stare at the walls. 'I guess I can see some Jackson Pollock influences in your work.'

'I stick to sculpture now,' he says. 'If I scrub the mold off first and do just one coat I should be able to finish the rooms by tomorrow. Without fixing the damp though, the mold will come back in a few weeks.'

'That's okay. This is a short-term fix. If we can pull it off then Aunt Kate can properly fix up the house later. All we have to do is make everything hold together for a week.'

'You mean we can stick everything together with chewing gum.'

Hmm, chewing gum.

'Danny? Could we fill the holes in the walls with gum?'

He shakes his head. 'No, that won't work. We tried it in our halls of residence to cover the nail holes we made in the plaster. Toothpaste is what you want for that.'

He goes back to his paintbrushes. I go to the bathroom to raid my makeup bag.

An hour later I survey my handiwork. The walls smell like toothpaste but they'll look okay with a coat of paint. It's a minty fresh renovation.

I'm even beginning to enjoy myself. With a bit of ingenuity and a lot more hard work, I feel like I'll honestly be able to tell Aunt Kate when I see her later that things are going to be all right.

CHAPTER FIVE

It's after midnight again before I crawl into Aunt Kate's bed with Mabel. I could move her into one of the other rooms once the stench of fresh paint wears off but I'd rather keep her with me. I love reaching out in the night to stroke her soft hair, or hear her rhythmic breathing on the pillow next to mine. I didn't know I could love someone this fiercely until I had her.

Aunt Kate always said she never wanted her own children (*What would I do with my own that I can't do with you, darling Lottie?*), but that made me a little sad. Then after Mum and Dad died, selfishly I was glad. It meant that Mabel and I didn't have to share her love with anyone else.

She continued to look after Mabel when I got back from Australia and I slept for two straight days. She quietly and efficiently took care of all the funeral arrangements, called the friends and made all the administrative changes that a death involves.

As we sat together on the sofa after the funeral,

surrounded by Mum and Dad's many friends, she quietly asked me if I wanted her to stay.

'Would you?'

'Lions couldn't chase me away if you want me here.'

'Yes, please.'

She moved into Mum and Dad's room and in those six months when she put her life on hold to help us learn to live ours again, she became as close to me as my own parents had been.

I'm going to do everything I can to help her now.

Danny is already in the kitchen when I come downstairs the next morning.

'Day two,' he says. 'Do you want some tea?'

'I could murder a cup, thanks.' I wince at myself. At least Mabel-the-Mimic is still asleep. Being big sister to the cat is proving tiring work.

He pours two large mugs and sits across from me at the long refectory table. I've got to say this for Aunt Kate. Her house might be falling down but she hasn't skimped on the décor. At least that gives us something to work with.

'Do you have everything here that you'll need for your cooking?'

'Sure. I can just make pasta every night, right?'

I laugh. 'Right. Imagine serving spag bol to a B&B critic. I've been thinking about that actually. Last night I ordered a bunch of stuff that should give us everything we need to impress them. It's supposed to arrive by tomorrow lunchtime. You have no idea how hard it was to find a company that could deliver here.'

I spent two hours in the conservatory with my teeth chattering before finding a shop online, called Posh

Food Fast, that can FedEx their food to us. 'We're not exactly within the Waitrose delivery area.'

'We're probably not even within the LIDL delivery area,' he says. 'Will you need me to get anything from the shops today?'

'I've made a list that should cover us for their whole stay.'

'Good, because everything will close tomorrow afternoon and probably won't open until the 27th.'

'That's what I figured. Can you go in to Rhyl today while Mabel and I visit Aunt Kate? You could do the shopping and then come back to collect us. If it's okay, I'll cook for us tonight after we get back from the hospital. I'd like to say thank you for helping me.'

Danny might be joking about the spag bol, but I'm not. Hopefully he likes pasta with ready-made sauce.

'You have paid me a packet to do it, but I'll accept your thanks too. Is there much left to do today?'

'Ha, what a naïve question. The answer is yes.' I pull the list from my bathrobe pocket. Where to start?

'I'm bored!' Mabel whines as I'm pulling all the dead weeds and flowers from the beds at the front of the house. My back aches and my arm muscles are protesting each stretch.

'Where's Mingus? I'm sure he'd like some company.'

'I can't find him.'

I'm not surprised. He lost his sense of humor when she tried combing his coat with her hairbrush.

'Go see if you can help Danny.'

'He sent me out here to help you.'

I smirk into the bushes. He's obviously dealt with children before. 'Okay, let me think a minute, and I can give you a job to do, okay?'

'A fun job?'

'Absolutely. Is there any other kind?'

Twenty minutes later Mabel is surrounded by a sea of silver at the dining room table. There must be fifty pieces scattered around the house, from candlesticks and ornate candelabra to delicate mirrors, hairbrushes, sugar tongs and decorative boxes. You name it and someone covered it in silver and sold it to Aunt Kate.

I feel a bit bad as I kiss my daughter's forehead and leave her there with pots of silver polish. But someone will have to do it and she does have those dexterous little fingers. Besides, it isn't exploitative child labor when you've given birth to the laborer.

'Do you have lights or anything for the front?' Danny asks as I rake years of dead leaves from under the overgrown bushes. We haven't found any clippers so Mr. Grey-Smythe and his family will have to accept our wild and rustic hedges.

'It would look a lot more Christmassy,' he continues. 'You could have a ready-made Christmas tree right here.'

Shit!

'We don't have a tree for inside,' I say. 'We can't host guests for Christmas without a Christmas tree. Is it too late to order one?'

He stares at me, smirking. 'Order one? Is that how they do it in London?'

As if I don't feel foolish enough without admitting that my parents ordered our Christmas tree from the same delivery service for more than a dozen years.

'I suppose you'd just go chop one down in the

forest then?'

'Generally, yes. Do you know where to find a saw?'

'In the garage, I guess.' My eye falls on the tree by the front door. 'Maybe we could cut this one down.'

'And leave the stump? I'm not sure your aunt would appreciate you chopping down her landscaping. We can find one in the wood.'

'Fine, then let me just get Mabel.' She'll love seeing a Christmas tree in its natural environment. It'll be like the time we went bird-watching in Regent's Park.

We're stomping through brambles half an hour later looking for two straight, tall trees for the parlor and the hall.

'Do you usually play jolly woodsman like this?' I call to Danny as he walks a bit ahead with the saw slung over his shoulder. He looks at home among the trees, casual, relaxed and competent. So different from my parents. They and their friends were uncomfortable when out of range of recycling facilities. Such a manly display is remarkable. Mabel isn't the only one impressed by our outing.

'Nah, usually I'd work this week and next so it's not worth bothering with a tree.'

'I guess a lot of people need taxis over the holidays.'

He shakes his head. 'I don't mean driving the taxi. I take two weeks off at the end of each year so that I can sculpt full-time. It's what I've always wanted to do. I used to nick the soap from our bathroom at home and carve it into tiny animals, drove my parents mad. So when it came time to decide on a course, art was the obvious choice. But it doesn't pay, so I fit it in around driving.'

'A taxi driver with the soul of an artist.' I smile. 'Do

you sell your sculptures and have exhibits and things like that?'

'Yeah, but like I said, I can't support myself yet. One day maybe. What do you do for work?'

'Oh, it's boring. I'm a software programmer, mostly for games.'

His eyes light up. 'That doesn't sound boring. Do you like it?'

'Well it pays the bills and I don't mind it. And I guess it's only boring if you're not a gamer.'

'What about you? Are you a gamer?'

I shrug. Despite working in the industry for five years, the gaming bug never really took hold. I much prefer curling up with a good book or crap telly.

'Mummy, look!' Mabel runs to a pretty pine and hugs it. 'Ouch.'

'Mind the needles.'

Her eyes widen at my caution.

'I don't mean real needles,' I add. 'The pine tree's leaves are called needles. I think that one might be a bit small.'

It's exactly Mabel's height.

'How about this one?' I say of the one beside it. 'It's pretty straight. What do you think, Danny?'

'Your job is to choose, mine is to chop. Say the word and it's ours.'

'Speaking of ours, are we trespassing?'

'Probably, but this seems like the kind of an emergency where trespassing's okay. So, will this be our Christmas tree?'

'I think so. It's tall enough. And that other one would work for the parlor.'

'Then stand back, ladies.'

Mabel springs to my side.

'Mabel,' he says. 'You've got the most important job. I'm going to saw and when you see it start to tip, you have to shout *timber*. Okay?'

She giggles.

'I'm not kidding. It's critical, so get ready.'

She giggles again and whispers, 'Tell me when, Mummy, okay, so I don't miss it?'

An hour later the Christmas trees are up in the hall and the parlor, thanks to Danny's handy homemade tree stands. They're bare of ornaments though.

'Let's have a look around for Aunt Kate's Christmas stash.'

We've already found decorations for Easter, Valentine's Day and the Queen's Jubilee squirreled away in the many cabinets in the house. If the worst comes to the worst we can hang the trees with bunting and call it a patriotic Christmas.

I don't believe in ghosts but I swear the house retains some of the character of its past inhabitants. It's easy to imagine women of a certain age in full stage makeup and flowing gowns draped on the sofas and chaises lounges while Ivan plays host, tipping ice cubes into gin and tonics.

Of course they probably wore track suits to the Tesco and did Zumba in the conservatory but I prefer the romantic ideal. It's not like they're around to tell me I'm wrong.

'Lottie, I found them,' Danny calls as he staggers downstairs with a large cardboard box. 'There's another one up there. It's not heavy, just awkward to carry. This one has the lights. If you want to check them I'll go get the other box.'

Mabel and I begin plugging in each of the dozen strings to make sure they work.

'This should be enough for both trees,' I say, winding the first string around from the top.

'If we space them carefully,' she adds.

I look at her. 'Do you remember Granddad saying that every year?'

'No, but you say it every year,' she says shyly. 'And then you say that Granddad always said it. Does it make you sad?'

'No, honey, it makes me happy to remember him.'

We've just put the lights on the first tree when Danny brings the other box down. 'Sorry for the delay but I had to take a phone call.'

I keep forgetting that he has his own life outside Aunt Kate's B&B.

'I think we've got plenty of decorations. Some look like antiques,' he says.

'I'm not surprised. Aunt Kate loves Christmas. She's going to be so unhappy to miss this one.'

I feel a little stab at my words. As I sat by her hospital bed last night, I kept wishing she'd open her eyes. It was very hard to remember that the drugs were keeping her in the coma. She'll sleep as long as the doctors want her to.

'We'll have Christmas with her when she wakes up, won't we Mummy?'

'Definitely, and she'll love how we've decorated the house. I bet it hasn't looked this good since- Can I see those, please, Mabel?'

She hands me the box of ornaments she's just picked up.

Oh, Mum.

It's an old fashioned ornament box, the kind from the fifties or sixties made of thin white cardboard with a cellophane window on the top and a dozen compartments for glass baubles. Whatever baubles once lived there are long gone though, replaced by others that were never a set.

They were my mother's.

Or duplicates at least. Every year Mum bought a new ornament for our tree. The little wooden drummer boy, the blown glass Christmas tree, the pom-pom snowman, they're all here. She must have bought two and sent one to Aunt Kate each year. After the accident, Celine made sure she packed ours in a separate box at home. They've stayed in the attic for the last three Christmases.

Now it's time to hang them again. 'Here, Mabel, you can hang this one.'

Carefully she selects a branch for the silver angel. 'It's beautiful. Is it a guardian angel?'

'I think it must be.'

CHAPTER SIX

I'm dead on my feet by the time Danny drives us back from the hospital that night. But a promise is a promise so, practically delirious, I stumble to the kitchen, over-boiled the pasta, pour over a jar of sauce and, as a small apology for my cooking, make up a batch of elderflower and ginger cordial for us all.

'Mummy, don't come in yet!' Mabel calls from behind the closed dining room door.

I do as I'm told, looking around the hall. It won't win any House Beautiful awards but it's not bad for two days' hard graft. I just hope the toothpaste holds up in the walls.

'Okay, you can come iiinnn,' she sings.

The dining room is beautiful. Two candelabra stand on the long sideboard against the back wall and pine boughs are tucked over the large gilded mirror above it. More boughs rest on the window sills and the freshly washed panes reflect the candlelight back into the room. The middle of the long dining table is illuminated too.

'We didn't use the tablecloth because I might spill on it,' Mabel says.

'Or I might spill on it,' Danny says.

'Most likely it'd be me though,' Mabel says. 'I am only seven.'

'You did a beautiful job. What a transformation.'

Danny smiles. 'I think it looks good enough for the reviewer, don't you?'

'If he's not impressed with this he'll have a heart of stone.' My tummy fizzes with excitement. We're going to pull this off!

I pour the cordial into three cut glass goblets and dish out our dinner. 'I'm sorry the food probably won't measure up to the surroundings, but as I said, cooking isn't my forte. That's why I'm paying you. Cheers.' I clink Mabel's and Danny's glasses. 'At least I know how to make good drinks.'

'This is delicious,' he says. 'Elderflower?'

'Yes, and ginger. If I'd remembered the lime I'd have added that. I'm glad you're impressed with the drinks. Remember that when you taste my cooking.'

'Oh I'm sure it's not bad.'

He takes a forkful.

'Hmm. Well. The drinks are good.'

Mabel catches my eye. 'I think it's just fine, Mummy, thank you.'

'Mabel,' Danny says, reddening. 'Where are my manners? Thank you, Lottie, for dinner. Everything is great.'

'Liar,' I say. 'But thank you.'

'Pants on fire,' murmurs Mabel into her spaghetti.

I feel a jolt as I watch Mabel happily chatting with

Danny. When I was first pregnant I worried about being a single mother, but when we moved in with Mum and Dad those worries faded. Mabel got to have two extra people who loved her. Aside from the occasional questions about her father she didn't seem to mind our modern family arrangement.

But did she, really?

As if reading my mind, Mabel says, 'Mummy, is Aunt Kate married?'

'Nope, she was never married.'

'But what about Uncle Ivan?'

She'd never met Ivan but Aunt Kate always talked about him like he was still around. 'They were very dear friends, but they weren't married. Uncle Ivan was a confirmed bachelor.'

'What's that?'

'It just means he wasn't the marrying kind.'

'Danny, are you the marrying kind?'

'Mabel,' I warn. Our financial arrangement doesn't give us the right to pry into his personal life.

'No, I've never been married.'

He forks in another mouthful of spaghetti. What a good sport.

'I guess nobody'd have me.'

I find that hard to believe, but Mabel seems to consider this. 'I guess nobody'd have Mummy either.'

Danny tries to cover his laugh with a cough, but fails.

She's not wrong though. Her father didn't stick around in the relationship for very long after I dropped the bombshell on him. I was devastated but, as I mentioned, I knew right away that I wanted Mabel.

I should give her father some credit though. He

might have bolted from our relationship but he did try to be a dad, of sorts. He was a sporadic presence in our lives for the first few years, but as much as I wanted Mabel to know him, every time he visited it opened the wound in my heart again. And Mabel was ambivalent towards him. As a toddler she didn't understand why this virtual stranger occasionally visited, expecting her to welcome him. His visits became more awkward over time until finally they stopped. So, after wishing for years that we could be a family, it was actually a relief by the time he moved to Thailand and left Mabel and me to get on with our lives. Knowing him he's probably living in a beach hut with a string of young women that he updates more often than he does his Facebook status.

'I do have a daughter though,' Danny says. 'She's eight and she lives all the way over in America.'

Ah, that explains why he's so good with Mabel.

'Is she like me?'

'Well, she is smart like you, and nice and pretty, so yes, I guess she is.'

'But she doesn't live with you?'

'Mabel, you must be getting tired,' I say, seeing the sadness in Danny's eyes. 'If you're finished eating, let's get your teeth brushed, okay? I'll come back down in a few minutes to help with the dishes.'

'That's okay, I can clear up and make us some tea.'

By the time I tuck Mabel into bed and return to the dining room, the table is laid with pretty teacups and saucers.

'Mabel is great,' Danny says, pouring my tea.

'She has her moments.' I sigh. 'She can really get on my nerves sometimes. Does it make me a bad mother to say that? Sometimes when I listen to everyone else talk about how perfect their children are, I do wonder if I'm just less maternal or if mine really is a pain in the arse.'

Danny smiles. 'She's just precocious because she's clever and, no, that doesn't make you a bad mother. People who act like their children can do no wrong are kidding themselves. Nobody's perfect, but most are okay.'

This makes me feel good. 'She is a good kid at heart and it hasn't always been easy for her. My parents died three years ago and she took it pretty hard. We all did.'

'That's really crap, I'm sorry.'

'It was total crap, but it's a little easier now. Aunt Kate was amazing. She came to live with us after it happened. That's why, now…'

'I understand. But you said she's recovering.'

I don't want to dwell in the shadowy corners of my imagination. Instead I nod. 'Tell me about your daughter.'

She lives with her mother, he says, in Austin Texas where she's from. She's an artist too, and they met in university. I can't help thinking that Danny's story mirrors mine and Mabel's. I wonder if her father ever misses her like Danny obviously misses his daughter.

'Do you get to see her?'

He fiddles with the delicate handle on his teacup. His big hands look ill-suited to such a delicate object.

'As often as I can get the money together for a flight. Her mother is good about me visiting. She was the one who wanted to move back to the US when Phoebe was two. Otherwise I'd see her more often.'

'So you're not together with Phoebe's mother

because of the distance?'

'Oh no,' he laughs. 'We're not together because we drove each other insane. She thought I was too intense and she never took anything seriously. We argued all the time. The best thing about our relationship was Phoebe. Luckily she got the right balance from both of us.' He sighs. 'I can't wait to see her again.'

I can't imagine being away from Mabel for weeks or months at a time. 'When will you go next?'

'Right after Christmas, thanks to you.'

So that's why he took up my offer.

'Then it was lucky I came along.'

'Very lucky.'

As we sit drinking our tea, a low rumble starts behind the dining room's back wall.

'That must be the 8.30 train,' I say, checking my watch. 'Right on time.'

The teacups begin to rattle in their saucers as the train closes in on us. It sounds like it might come through the house.

White flecks begin raining down on to the table. Against the dark wood they look at first like terrible dandruff, but larger pieces fall as the train passes. A chunk the size of a fifty pence piece splashes into my teacup.

'Holy shit,' says Danny. 'That ceiling is about to come down.'

As the sound recedes I survey the debris strewn across the table top. 'I doubt my toothpaste is going to help here. We can't let the reviewer see this. What'll we do? The only other place to eat is the kitchen... I don't suppose we could we make a chef's table there and let them watch you cook.'

'No way! I mean they'll have to have Christmas dinner in here. Otherwise it's not very Christmassy. The ceiling only seems to cave in because of the train. You'll just have to keep them out of here at 8.30. Otherwise the house looks fine.'

The list of things we need to hide from the reviewer is getting longer than those we want to show him.

'Oh sure, it might look fine,' I say. 'We just can't let anyone take a shower, sit here in the evening or try to use their mobile inside the house.'

I'm kidding myself. The reviewer won't judge the house on cosmetics alone. It has to meet all his needs. I'm guessing a shower is on that list.

I wish Aunt Kate were here. She'd know what to do.

'I don't know if we can do this,' I say. 'There's still a lot wrong with the house.'

'What would your aunt say?'

I laugh. 'She'd say "Come on, girl, if at first you don't succeed, then try, try again. Rome wasn't built in a day" and about half a dozen other platitudes that don't quite fit. She's right though. Not trying would be worse than failing. Maybe if we think of everything that could be a problem and then find a way around those things, there'll still be a chance. Starting with the train. We could use the dining room earlier in the day. Can we serve lunch each day instead of having the main meal in the evening? We could just make sandwiches for later on.'

'Tea at teatime.' he nods. 'That might work.'

I have to stop thinking about what we can't do and think about what we can do.

'There are those beautiful bathtubs in all the bathrooms. Could you take the shower extensions off the taps, and maybe get the mounts off the walls? I think I have enough extra toothpaste to fill the holes. Then at least if someone flushes, nobody will die.'

'You can tell everyone that mobile phones are restricted to the conservatory. Make it sound like it's in keeping with the ambiance. I can make sure the fire is always lit in there so that it's warm.'

'This is starting to sound like a Victorian house. All we need are servants running up and down the back stairs tugging their forelocks and curtsying.'

Wait a minute...

'Why not?' I say. 'Why not make this a Victorian Christmas? We're practically there anyway.'

Then we brush the debris from the table and stay in the dining room until after midnight again, working through all the details.

CHAPTER SEVEN

Mabel comes downstairs on Christmas Eve morning wearing her favorite blue tutu. I've been up for hours already trying to find enough duvets that aren't coated in Mingus hair. I did find enough extra candlesticks and candles to put some in each room. We're going to stretch the Victorian theme as far as we possibly can. If I find any brass bed-warmers or stocking caps I'm definitely laying them out for our guests.

'You look beautiful, Mabel.'

'Well we have to look our best for our guests, don't we?'

I stare down at myself. My jeans are covered with paint. Mold and lord knows what else streak my once-white top. Even if I could get them clean, Mabel is right. I don't look fit to be a twenty-first century B&B host, let alone a Victorian lady.

Unfortunately when I'd packed my bag at three a.m. to come here, I wasn't thinking about impressing a B&B reviewer and his family.

'Morning,' she says to Danny, who's on his knees in the hall rubbing the floorboards with tan shoe polish. There was no floor varnish among Aunt Kate's paint pots but for some reason she has an entire box of shoe polish in the closet. Danny is touching up the spots where we had to clean up his paint splatters with nail varnish remover. For someone who claims to be a sculptor he really doesn't seem to have great hand-eye coordination.

'Can we have scrambled eggs this morning?' Mabel asks.

'Sure, if we've got eggs.' He looks at me.

Oh god, I forgot all about the chickens!

'I've just got to check something outside, okay? Mabel, do you think Mingus is awake yet?'

My question sends her rushing off to find the cat while I hurry outside, hoping I haven't accidentally killed Aunt Kate's flock through neglect.

The back garden is wild and overgrown with once-manicured hedges and the uncut grass is flattened and streaked brown by the Welsh winter. It looks pretty grim but we don't have time now for any more gardening. Our guests are due at two pm.

My feet squelch in the wet undergrowth as I stomp to the crumbling garage, behind which I spy the chicken run. At one end is a hen house but I don't see any hens.

Creeping into the pen, I peek into the hut's doorway.

A dozen sharp beaks gnash in my face and two dozen beady eyes stare me down as the birds erupt into a chorus of threatening clucks and squawks. Naturally I scream my head off and run back to the house.

'Danny, what do you know about chickens?'

'I know how to eat them,' he says.

'It may come to that if our food doesn't arrive today. Cook said Don't forget the chickens in her email. I assume that means they lay eggs and might need feeding. Could you please go see if there are any eggs? They're just out back behind the garage.'

'If you were just out there why didn't you…?'

'I had a quick look but they seemed angry.'

'You're frightened of chickens.'

'Don't you remember *The Birds*? I was traumatized by that film. They go for the eyes.'

He shakes his head, mumbling, 'Then I'd better watch out for rampaging chickens.'

He's back ten minutes later, his eyes and entrails intact. 'The chickens are fed, and look what we've got!'

I peer into his basket. 'Those aren't eggs are they?'

Some are round, some oblong, others as tiny as grapes.

'Don't let the chickens hear you say that. They're very proud of their efforts.'

'Well if they're happy then I shan't complain. It's not like I can lay any myself.'

The shops in the village will be closed for Christmas by now anyway. They'll have to do.

Danny goes, whistling, to the kitchen to cook us an omelet.

The FedEx driver turns up just before noon, as grumpy as those in London always seem to be. But at least Posh Food Fast hasn't let us down.

Danny looks over my shoulder as I unpack. 'Mmm, look at this!' I say.

'Tinned tuna?'

'Psh, you need glasses. It's caviar! I wasn't sure if they'd be able to get it. It was out of stock on the website. Ooh and look at this beef.'

There's also a whole salmon and smoked salmon and kippers and Christmas pudding. My mouth is watering just thinking about the feast ahead. Of course, technically being the hired help, we'll be eating the ample leftovers, but good food is good food.

'We can offer oatmeal or cooked breakfast in the mornings, okay? I wonder if I should write up a little menu to hand out. That'd be a nice touch. And I thought we could have the salmon for dinner today and the beef for tomorrow. Maybe you can make a nice sauce to go with the salmon and do something special with the carrots and potatoes. We've got lots of bread for sandwiches later. You'll do them with the crusts cut off, right?'

'Err, all right, if you want. How do I cook the salmon?'

'However you want. You're the chef! I'm just going to check on Mabel and get out of these clothes before everyone arrives. I'll let you make a start. We should probably eat around three.'

After making Mabel and Danny triple-promise and cross their hearts not to flush the loo, I have a quick shower. Then I survey my suitcase for the millionth time, hoping my clothes have turned couture in the night. I've got only jeans, tee shirts and a few worse-for-wear jumpers.

Rupert Grey-Smythe and his family will just have to overlook my appearance. I can't magic up an outfit out of thin air…

Although maybe I can find one in Aunt Kate's closet. She's bigger than me but if there's a dress that won't make me look like a sixty-year-old B&B owner, I might be able to adapt it.

My heart sinks when I fling open the closet doors. There are loads of wide legged trousers and long colorful tunics, but not a single dress.

Unless Mabel lets me borrow her tutu, I'll have to make do with what's in the closet. A belt will at least hold up the trousers. At worst there's clothesline downstairs.

The closet is bigger than I thought. It seems to run along the entire length of the wall.

I get my phone out and shine the light into its murky depths.

What greets me takes my breath away.

'Danny! Mabel, come in here!'

I pull the tunics and trousers off the rails and fling them on the bed.

Mabel has Mingus clasped to her chest as she runs in. Danny is close behind.

'What do you think of these?'

Half an hour later, I look every inch the Victorian lady (as long as you don't see my trainers beneath my dress). Aunt Kate's opera frocks, made of rich dark velvets and silks, are a bit wrinkled but unbelievably beautiful.

And it seems she wasn't the only singer to be paid in clothes. Ivan's knee breeches and embroidered waistcoat are big for Danny but the clothesline sorted him out.

'You look like a princess!' cries Mabel.

I drape a deep purple embroidered shawl over her

small shoulders. 'Would you like to wear this?'

'You do look good,' Danny says. 'Whereas I feel like a prat.'

'Oh come now, you could be Caruso himself.'

He doesn't look too sure.

'They're here!' Mabel shouts from the parlor window where she can see the driveway. 'They've got a lot of bags.'

Danny and I go out to greet them.

'Mr. Grey-Smythe?' I look between the two men taking luggage out of the boot.

'Yes, that's me. Please call me Rupert.' The taller man shakes my hand. 'Are you Kate?'

'Oh, no, I'm not. I'm her niece Lottie Crisp. It's a pleasure to meet you. Unfortunately my aunt has been in an accident and she's not able to be here.'

His brow creases with concern. 'I'm sorry to hear that. I hope she's all right?'

'Yes, she'll be fine, thanks.'

'Did I miss a memo somewhere?' he asks, scanning my dress.

'Ah, yes, well. Welcome to your Victorian Christmas!'

I bob into a little curtsey like they do on Downton Abbey.

'This is Danny, our chef.'

Danny just nods. 'Can I help you with your bags?' he asks.

'Thank you, yes. Hugo, leave those. The man will get them.'

Rupert strides toward the front door as I hurry to beat him to it.

His nose twitches as he enters the hall.

'It smells of shoe polish,' he says.

'Uh, yes, it's a complimentary service. You can just leave your shoes outside your door in the evening and we'll polish them. We'll take care of everything for you here.'

He nods.

'Yes, well, as I said, welcome to your Victorian Christmas. And you are?' I stick my hand out to the forty-something slender woman who hasn't cracked a smile since she arrived.

She doesn't bother making eye contact when she speaks. 'Prunella, Rupert's sister.' She waves her hand at the others. 'These are my twins Oscar and Amanda and my husband Hugo.'

The children look around Mabel's age, both pale and slim like their parents. In fact, Prunella and Hugo could be twins themselves with their beaky noses, close-set watery blue eyes and very high foreheads. Rupert, on the other hand, though slender like his sister, is darker with strong but not sharp features that assemble into a pleasing, if austere, countenance.

Hugo scans me up and down as he offers me his soft damp hand.

'Have you got Sky?' Prunella asks.

'No, I'm sorry, there's no television.'

'Mother!' says Oscar, glaring at me. 'How are we supposed to watch Bad Santa without a TV?'

'Never mind, darling, we'll watch it on the computer. You do have fast broadband, right?'

Her look dares me to disappoint her again.

'There's 3g in the conservatory.'

'Rupert,' she whines, 'I told you this would be the

middle of nowhere.'

'I suppose it's meant to be rustically charming, Pru.'

This isn't the start I hoped for. 'It will be charming, but I promise you it won't be rustic.'

'We'll make the best of it, Pru,' says Hugo.

'Oh do shut up, Hugo, you always say that. I want a bath now. We've been traveling all day to get here. Where's my room? And my luggage?'

Danny is just struggling in with all the bags.

'I'll show you upstairs then. Your rooms are all together on the first floor. You're going to love our bathtubs. As part of the service, we'll run your baths for you, so that all you'll have to do is step into the soothing water when you're ready. After all, ladies and gentlemen didn't prepare their own baths in Victorian days. There's a button in each of your rooms by the door that rings a bell in the kitchen. Just press that when you want anything and someone will be right up.'

'Whew,' I say when I get back to the kitchen after drawing Prunella's bath. Danny is pulling food from the fridge and larder. 'This is going to be hard work. Is everything under control here?'

'Controlled chaos, thanks.' He wipes his brow. Pots are boiling on the hob and the work surfaces look as if there's been a mass vegetable suicide.

'Okay, if you're sure.'

The bell for Hugo and Prunella's room tinkles.

'I'm sorry I told them about those service buttons. I'll go see what they want.'

Upstairs I knock on the closed door.

'Come in,' says Hugo.

'Hi, did you want something?'

He's lying on the bed in his bathrobe.

'Oh, excuse me.'

'Ah, Lottie, yes. I wondered if I could have a brandy? I'd like to relax while Prunella is in the bath. She'll be ages.'

'I'll check downstairs. Dinner will be in about an hour. You can go down to the dining room whenever you'd like. Is that all right?'

'Yes, that's fine. Oh, and please don't think my wife is ungrateful. Today is just a bad day. We're very much looking forward to our stay, and I do appreciate your costumes very much. Yes,' he says, his eyes flickering to my chest. 'Very much.'

'I'll see if I can find that brandy.'

And some pepper spray.

He's a bit creepy. I hate to think what he'll be like after a few drinks…

Oh no. I haven't. Have I? I have.

I can't believe I forgot to put wine on Danny's shopping list. Or brandy or anything stronger than the elderflower cordial we had last night.

I hurry to the kitchen. 'Danny, you haven't run across a stash of wine, have you? Or spirits? Anything?'

'No, why?'

'I completely forgot to get any alcohol.'

Of course they'll want to drink. It's Christmas. And they'll need alcohol just to put up with each other.

'How could you forget something like that?' He brushes a lock of his unruly hair out of his eyes.

'Because I don't drink.'

After the drunk driver turned my world upside down, the thought of taking even a sip is too unappealing.

'Hugo has already asked for brandy. They're going

to expect wine at the very least. The shops are closed now, aren't they?'

I know the answer.

'Well,' he says. 'I do have something at home, but you may not like it.'

'It doesn't really matter if I like it, as long as we've got booze for the guests.'

'Then I can run home and get a few bottles. You've still got lots of that cordial, right? We'll use that to cut the- as mixers. Can you please keep an eye on the potatoes and take them off the heat when they're ready?'

'Sure thing. Thanks, Danny.'

At least you can't overcook potatoes.

CHAPTER EIGHT

'You've overcooked the potatoes,' Danny says half an hour later, poking the mush with a fork. 'Did you check the carrots?'

As instructed, I haven't taken my eyes off the potato pot. 'You didn't say anything about the carrots.'

He frowns when he peers into the pot. 'I guess we'll add enough butter and salt to make up for it.' Holding up a green bottle, he adds, 'By the time they get through this, they won't be able to taste anything anyway.'

'What is it?' There's no label on the bottle.

'This is gin.' He pulls another bottle from his bag. 'And this is brandy. Just make sure you always serve it in very small quantities. Whatever you do, never leave the bottle with the guests.'

'And why aren't there any labels on the bottles?'

'I don't bother having labels made. I know which is which.'

'As long as it doesn't blind anyone.'

'My eyesight is perfect.'

'Then let's mix one with the cordial.'

I start pouring the gin into the pitcher I used for our drinks last night, but Danny grabs my hand.

'Hey, hey, stop. You'll kill them. Seriously, you need about a dessert spoonful for each glass, that's all. You'd better let me do it.'

Everyone is assembled in the dining room waiting for their lunch. Prunella's mood wasn't improved by her bath and the twins are rocking back and forth in their chairs, absorbed in a game of who-can-break-it-first. At least Hugo has his clothes on.

'Here we are!' I say.

The tureens of mash and carrots (also mash) are heavy in my arms.

Then a very nervous-looking Danny comes in with the steaming main course.

'We'll leave you to enjoy your lunch but do let us know if you need anything. Would everyone like a drink? There's also a non-alcoholic cordial for the children.'

'Where's the wine?' Prunella asks.

'Oh, well, we've made a special drink instead, and it's really delicious.'

'It's what the upper classes had at Christmas,' Danny says as he pours glasses for everyone.

Hugo nods like he knows this already.

'Thank you,' says Rupert. 'We'll let you know if we need anything.'

I fight the urge to curtsey. It's the damn dress.

'Wait a second,' says Hugo. 'Is that prosciutto wrapped around the salmon?'

'No, it's salmon,' says Danny, looking at me as if to say *What kind of nutter wraps salmon in prosciutto?*

My look glares back: Who the hell wraps salmon in more salmon?

'Ah, yes, our salmon-in-salmon recipe,' I say. 'We've researched the menus of the era and were surprised at some of them too, but they're authentic.' My face reddens. Surely they don't believe all this bullshit.

But Hugo is already downing his gin cordial and Prunella has her fingers on her temples. Something tells me she has a lot of bad days.

'And here's the gravy!' Mabel says, setting it on the table.

'Gravy on salmon?' Rupert asks, pouring a bit on the side of his plate. 'Beef?'

'It's good on the mash,' the girl twin, Amanda, says, talking with her mouth full. 'It tastes like Mother's.'

'Gravy granules?' I mouth at Danny.

'And I suppose the carrots are pureed like this because Victorians lost their teeth early,' Rupert says.

That sounds at least as good as the excuse I'm about to come up with.

'Hmm, I'm not sure I've got a Victorian palate,' he continues. 'But I do appreciate the effort. Thank you.'

We rush out before they can ask any more questions.

'You used all the smoked salmon?' I hiss to Danny when we're safely back in the kitchen.

'You said to cook the salmon.'

'You don't cook smoked salmon. You eat it as it is. Now what are we supposed to do for their tea tonight?'

'I wouldn't eat it as it is. It looked slimy and raw.'

I'm beginning to doubt Danny's culinary skills, but

considering that I've made baby food of the veg, I'm not any better.

Upstairs, the tile floor is soaking wet from Prunella's bath and her towel is in a heap beside the loo. The messy cow.

As I mop the floor I hope the family won't want too many baths. I know the twins won't. They're the same age as Mabel and she acts like soap and water might kill her. It's a daily fight to keep her non-infectious.

We just have time to run to the hospital to see Aunt Kate before we need to prepare tea, so we leave everyone in the parlor with a stack of board games and newspapers. The twins' fury over the lack of telly is soon forgotten when they catch sight of Mingus. That poor cat.

Danny stays behind to boil the eggs for sandwiches, throwing me his car keys.

'Just don't hit anything, please,' he adds after telling me the trick to coaxing the car out of third gear.

'How is she?' I ask Doctor Londergan when she comes in to Aunt Kate's room. 'Any better?'

She smiles. 'Yes, in fact. I want to keep her on the medication for another day or so and then we should be able to reverse the coma.'

'Can you tell about possible brain damage?'

'All the tests we've run look clear, so that's a good sign. How are you holding up?'

Her concern threatens to undo me. I don't have time for a meltdown now. 'I'm fine. The guests have arrived at the house, so it's been a little crazy.'

'But it's going to be fine, Aunt Kate,' I say, in case

she can hear me. I take her hand. 'They're all settled in and they've had their lunch. So you don't have to worry, okay?'

I squeeze her hand, remembering too late that she can't squeeze back.

We make it back to the B&B without stalling the car. Perhaps if there's a bit of money left over from Danny's ticket to America he might think about upgrading it from death trap to load of junk.

The hard-boiled eggs are cooling in a bowl beside the sink. I slice into the first one. Well, I say slice. It's more of a sawing motion.

'How long did you boil the eggs?'

'Not long. Half an hour or so. Are they cooked?'

'Oh they're cooked.' We can use them in defense of the house if necessary. 'They're hard as rocks.'

'Really? I didn't want to under-cook them.'

'Mission accomplished.' Unless the hens have gone into extra production, there aren't enough for a second batch. 'Let me think.'

We've got to have something to feed everyone with their tea. I haven't the faintest idea how to bake and, judging by Danny's efforts so far, neither has he. That leaves sandwiches, but with no smoked salmon and now no eggs, what are we supposed to make?

The bell over the door rings. They must have found the button in the parlor.

'The Master calls. I'll be right back. Meanwhile try to think of something we can use for sandwiches.'

'Sure,' he says. 'Is it okay if I run home quickly?'

'Have you got something at home that we could use?'

He frowns. 'I'm a bachelor living alone. They won't want pot noodles.'

'Right. Wishful thinking. You may as well do whatever you need to do at home. You don't need to be back here till six. I'll try to think of something.'

Prunella is prostrate on one of the sofas in front of the fire with her hand over her eyes, while the twins take turns throwing the Yahtzee dice at each other from five paces.

'Is everything all right?'

'I have a splitting headache,' says Prunella. 'Have you got any tablets?'

'Sure, I'll just go get them.'

'Bring in some more of that drink, will you?' Hugo asks. 'Actually I can help you carry the glasses.'

He hops up from the chair, swaying slightly as he does so.

'Hugo, I'm sure she's perfectly capable of carrying a tray by herself. Honestly, it is what she does.'

It's not worth pointing out that what I *do* is design gaming software for brats like hers.

'To tell the truth, I don't mind getting away from the family for a while,' Hugo says as he follows me to the kitchen. 'We were supposed to go to Tanzania and they're still angry with Rupert for bringing us to Wales instead. But it's his dosh so I can't really blame him for choosing a free holiday over one that'd cost a packet.'

'Free?' Aunt Kate doesn't charge very much for her rooms but they aren't free.

'All expenses paid, Rupert said. I guess that's because your aunt needs the rating. She's comped our whole stay.'

Terrific. Not only are we killing ourselves to please these pompous farts, we're doing it for free.

I can feel him come up behind me as I reach into the cabinet for glasses. He's standing way too close. This is a rural kitchen, not a rush-hour Tube train.

I should grind my heel into his foot but Aunt Kate pops into my head. If she has comped Rupert's whole stay then it tells me just how much she feels she needs his rating. As much as I'd love to castrate Hugo, I can't throw away her only chance.

He grasps the counter on either side of me as I turn with the glasses. 'I couldn't help but notice the way you looked at me earlier.'

Yes, with utter contempt.

'I'm sorry, I-'

'Ssh, you don't have to be sorry.'

As his blubbery lips dart towards mine I get a whiff of his foul breath.

'Jesus!' he shouts, with his upper lip clenched between my teeth.

Oh my god. I've bitten the reviewer's brother-in-law.

But then he smiles (when I release his lip) and shrugs. 'Oh I see, you like to play hard to get.'

Behind Hugo I see a movement.

'I didn't mean to interrupt.'

Rupert is standing in the doorway, watching us.

CHAPTER NINE

Hugo springs backward at the sound of his brother-in-law's voice. 'No, I don't think there's anything in your eye,' he says. 'I can't see anything.'

'Thanks. Actually it feels better now.'

My heart is hammering.

'Would you like a drink, Rupert?' I ask.

'No, thank you. I was just checking on when tea would be ready. I've got some work to do.'

'Would seven be all right? We'll serve it in the parlor. I've just got to get some headache tablets for Prunella.'

I rush from the room, leaving the two men staring each other down.

What must Rupert think? They've been here less than three hours and I've just rounded off an afternoon of bathtub gin and a questionable lunch with a romantic interlude in the arms of his sister's husband.

Unless one of his rating categories includes staff promiscuity, I've just put Aunt Kate's livelihood in jeopardy.

'Are you okay?' Danny asks when he returns at six on the dot. 'You look weird.'

Humiliation is coursing through me. I don't want to tell Danny what happened in the kitchen.

'Oh I'm fine. I think this corset is too tight, that's all. I've been thinking about the sandwich situation. We can serve some of the caviar for the adults and make peanut butter and jam sandwiches for the twins. Aunt Kate has about three jars of it in the larder and Mabel goes nuts for the stuff, so I'm sure the twins will love it.'

'That's going to be hard to spin as Victorian,' he says.

'We can't be perfect. At least they won't go hungry. Just toast the bread for the caviar. With a little lemon it'll be great. Very decadent. I'll make another batch of drinks.'

Maybe if Hugo drinks enough he'll pass out before he can lunge at me again.

'I've got to turn down everyone's beds while they're all downstairs, and restock the bathrooms. You're okay making the sandwiches and the tea?'

He nods, already counting out slices of bread.

It's only taken a few hours for the parlor to look like a bomb's hit it. The twins have pulled nearly every book from the shelves. The cushions are off all the sofas and unoccupied chairs and Oliver is throwing the Monopoly money in the air to watch it rain down over everything.

Danny noses the tea trolley through the door.

'Look, darlings, tea!' Hugo says. His earlier sexual assault seems forgotten but I'm pleased to see that his lip is swollen. Prunella hasn't noticed, but then she hasn't really paid him any attention since they arrived.

Rupert is staring at the trolley.

'Is everything okay?' I ask before I can stop myself. What if he outs me like a real-life edition of Cluedo? *It was Ms. Crisp in the kitchen with a romantic embrace.*

'I was just remembering my Granny's tea trolley. It looked just like that.'

Probably with better food though.

'Do you remember it, Prunella?'

'I remember that she stank,' she says, shifting to a sitting position. 'I don't know why you insist on deifying her, Rupert.'

'I don't deify her, Pru-, I just have good memories of being with her. Maybe if you let yourself feel anything but dissatisfaction, you would too.'

'You can be ridiculous sometimes. I'll just have a cup of tea,' she says to me. 'White. I'm not hungry after that lunch.'

'Of course,' I say, pouring her a cup and wishing they wouldn't bicker in front of "the help". 'Would everyone like tea?'

'I'll have some more of that cocktail, if there's any going,' Hugo says.

I'm not about to leave the safety of the room again. 'Danny, could you please make a pitcher?'

'What's this?' Amanda demands as she picks up a sandwich.

'It's peanut butter and jam,' I say. 'My daughter loves them and I thought…'

Her tongue darts into the side of the sandwich.

'Yuck, I hate it!' She throws it back on the plate.

'I hate it too!' cries Oliver, on sight alone. 'I'm not eating it.'

'You don't have to eat it, darlings. They'll make whatever you want.'

'Well actually…'

'Do you want to try a special one?' Danny says smoothly as he returns with a fresh pitcher of blinding cocktail. 'Children aren't usually allowed to have these. But since it is Christmas I think you could…' He seems to reconsider. 'Well, maybe you're not ready for one.'

'Yes, I want one!' says Oliver.

'Me too, give it to me now!'

Danny sighs. 'Well all right, but you're very lucky.' He hands a sandwich from the second plate to each child.

What are those?

Amanda and Oliver look unsure as they sniff the toasted bread. Then Amanda, in her trademark move, sticks her tongue into the side. Her eyes widen. She tears open the sandwich and licks it clean before throwing the spittle-slicked toast back on the plate.

'I want another one.'

Oliver levers his sandwich open. 'Me too. I like it!'

Well at least they'll get to eat something.

'I'll just go get the caviar,' I say.

'No need, it's right there. In the sandwiches.'

Amanda and Oliver are stuffing caviar sandwiches into their foul little mouths.

'Wow, that's impressive,' says Hugo. 'They're usually very fussy eaters. It looks like we'll need more sandwiches.'

Sighing, I go to the kitchen to make a hundred quid

worth of caviar into sandwiches for greedy children.

Rupert follows me.

'Lottie, may I have a quiet word please?'

'Listen, Rupert, that wasn't what you—'

'It's about the stockings,' he says.

I'm not wearing stockings, so he can't possibly take issue with my attire. Is he one of those sexist men who think women deserve what they get just because they're not dressed in floor-length potato sacks?

'Just what are you implying?'

'I'm not implying anything. Your aunt told me she'd have stockings for the children's gifts tonight. If you give them to me, please, I can put them in Prunella's room.'

Of course, it's Christmas Eve. I have a stocking for Mabel too, easily portable gifts that I've carefully chosen over the past few months in anticipation of our visit. Father Christmas is leaving her big gifts at home for when we return.

But I haven't the faintest idea where Aunt Kate might have stashed the twins' stockings. There weren't any in the boxes of ornaments we found.

I can't even give him a pair of my socks. They wouldn't be big enough.

'I'll just get them for you. Be right back!'

'You can leave them in Prunella's room. Thank you.'

Upstairs I tear through all of Aunt Kate's drawers but there isn't even a leftover sock of Ivan's, let alone any Christmas stockings.

So I don't really have any choice in the matter.

'Danny?' I call sweetly into the parlor. 'Can I see you out here for a minute, please?'

We throw ourselves, exhausted, on the sofas after everyone has retired to their rooms and Mabel is in bed. She wasn't at all disappointed that the twins turned their noses up at the peanut butter. We gorged on the sweet and savory sandwiches. The poor thing is probably upstairs now on a sugar high, trying to fall asleep so that Father Christmas can come.

Music drifts quietly from the record player in the corner. Aunt Kate's collection of classical music and operatic favorites fill an entire library shelf, giving us all the Callas, Carrera and Pavarotti we could want.

'That went okay, considering,' Danny says, rubbing his bare legs. He'll have a cold drive home without his socks.

'It could hardly have gone worse! It's probably wrong to hate children, right?'

'Not those children. They deserve a slap. Along with their parents.'

'You did very well with them though. You've got a knack with kids.'

'It helps to have your own.'

'You miss her.'

He nods. 'I think about her all the time. I'd move to America if I could, but that's not realistic. Without a way to work there legally, it would be a precarious way to live. I want to be a more stable influence in Phoebe's life, not a less stable one. It has to stay like this for a while, but now that she's getting older, she'll soon get to stay with me during her holidays.'

The joy in his face makes me grin too.

'What about Mabel's father?' he asks. 'Is he in the picture?'

'No, he erased himself when I fell pregnant.' I give

him the short answer. After all I've known him for less than forty-eight hours, even if it feels a lot longer than that.

'We've been okay, Mabel and I. We had my parents until three years ago, and Celine.'

'Ah the mythical Celine you keep mentioning. She does sound incredible.'

'She is. She's part of our family.'

He watches me from beneath his mop of hair. 'You say that, but can anyone you're paying really be part of the family? I don't mean to say that you don't love her, but at the end of the day she is your employee. If something went wrong you could fire her. You can't do that with family. You're stuck with them through thick and thin, whether or not you want to be.'

'I'm sure it started out as a financial arrangement with my parents but she's been with us since I was small, so she is part of my family.'

'Even though you pay her to cook and clean for you so you don't have to do it.'

I don't like his tone one bit. 'I'm not some spoilt silly rich woman you know. If you must know, we actually have very little extra money. Celine lives rent-free and we pay her a stipend.'

But that doesn't make it sound any better. What I mean is that, because she's part of the family, we all take care of each other.

Why am I being so defensive anyway? It doesn't matter what Danny thinks of us.

'You can go home now,' I say, pushing the discomfort from my mind. 'Can you be back by eight for breakfast?'

'You're the boss.'

'I didn't mean-'

'Good night, Lottie.'

He crosses the room in just a few seconds until he's towering over me.

'Happy Christmas.' He leans down and kisses my cheek, and I feel the warmth of his lips long after he's left for home.

CHAPTER TEN

Sleep doesn't come easily and it's not because I'm waiting for Father Christmas. I've got visions of Danny dancing in my head. Something about his vulnerability when he talks about his daughter tugs at my heart in a way it hasn't been tugged in years. So it's a shame that he thinks I'm a self-centered Londoner who exploits my "help".

And even if it has started to seem like we're just two friends together in this charade, the fact remains that he's drawing a salary to be here.

It's just past six a.m. when I finally admit defeat. Sleeplessness has won. Mabel stirs when I crawl out from under the duvet. I freeze. There's no way she'll go back to sleep this morning, not with a stocking full of presents waiting for her at the foot of our bed.

But she swallows in her sleep and turns over with a sigh. I don't risk kissing her.

'I love you, Mabel,' I whisper instead.

When I see the black shoes in the hallway, I have to

laugh. Rupert has taken me up on my offer to polish them. But my smile turns to a frown as I bend to pick them up.

Oh no. Please say he hasn't. Tentatively I give them a sniff.

He has.

Mingus has weed in Rupert's lace-ups.

That damn cat!

How does one clean cat wee out of leather shoes? Even Martha Stewart would struggle with that one.

Rupert won't appreciate wet shoes so I can't wash them. But I've got to get the smell out somehow.

I rush to the basement looking for anything that might help. Bleach? No, can't get them wet. Soap powder could help soak up the wee, at least. But would that leave a white residue? Then he'd think I'd been doing lines on his insoles. And if his feet became sweaty he might end up with bubbles in his shoes.

My gaze falls upon a bottle of Febreeze on the shelf above the washer. Ah, the miracle spray, savior of many a morning-after-curry W.C. and student who hasn't got around to washing his clothes.

Blotting a cloth inside each shoe first, I soak up as much of Mingus as possible before giving each one a blast.

It seems to be working, although Rupert's shoes now smell of Febreeze.

I take them into the kitchen and give them the polish he wanted in the first place.

Now they smell of shoe polish and air freshener. He's definitely going to be suspicious of that, but it's better than the alternative.

Mingus rubs against my leg, purring like he hasn't

just urinated in our guest's brogues.

'Bad cat!'

He looks perfectly innocent.

'Oh I suppose now you think I ought to feed you? For that little stunt, you're getting chicken for breakfast.'

He sniffs at the dish and turns away. His disdain is absolute.

Damn cat.

As I'm putting the rest of his food packets away I see Aunt Kate's spice cabinet. Which makes me wonder…

Twenty minutes later, Rupert's shoes smell deliciously of cloves, and faintly of shoe polish. He'll waft Christmas cake with every step today. Happy Christmas, Rupert.

I creep back upstairs to see if Mabel is awake.

'Good morning, Mummy,' she says when I open the door. She has her stocking clasped to her chest.

'Happy Christmas, Mabel! I see Father Christmas was here.'

'You didn't wake up either when he came in?'

Solemnly I shake my head. 'I didn't see him.'

'I wonder how he always sneaks past us? He must be very quiet.'

'Would you like to open your presents? Remember, the ones from me are at home, and I bet Father Christmas left the big presents there too, so that we don't have to carry them back on the train.'

'He's very considerate. Is Danny awake yet?'

'He doesn't sleep here, honey. He has his own house, remember?'

'But he could sleep here if he wanted to, right? That

would be all right with you, wouldn't it?'

What is she asking? 'You like Danny, don't you?'

'Oh he is a good egg. I like him very much… do you like him, Mummy?'

'Of course I do. He's a very nice man, and he's helping us a lot, isn't he?'

'Oh Mummy.' She rolls her eyes. 'I don't mean do you like him. I mean do you like him. Because he likes you.'

'What makes you say that?'

'Because he told me,' she says as a small green parcel at the top of the stocking grabs her attention. 'Should I open this one first?'

I can't pump my seven-year-old for information, much as I want to ask her exactly what Danny has said.

We keep our squeals to a minimum as Mabel tears through her stocking. Since we're not sure when the twins will get to open their gifts, we make a pact to keep her early morning bonanza a secret until later. Hopefully that'll avoid a double tantrum if they're made to wait until after lunch.

'I'll just go have a quick bath while everyone is still asleep, okay? Danny'll be here soon.'

'Okay, Mummy, I'll go find Mingus. I think he might like to play with this.'

Of all the gifts I've carefully chosen over the past six months, gifts I was really excited about, like the silver charm bracelet and wild animal stencil art box and LEGO Architecture Big Ben, it's the pencil with googly eyes and blue feather hair that she loves most.

Next year Father Christmas is shopping at Poundland.

'Mingus should have a Christmas too,' she

continues, bouncing off the bed.

Mingus should have a kick in the backside.

I creep to the bathroom. Every extra minute that Rupert's family stays behind closed doors is precious. I don't know how Aunt Kate does this for a living.

Flushing the loo, I go to wash my hands.

That's when I hear a rattling in the floor.

Oh no. I forgot to wait the five minutes prescribed by Cook.

Turning slowly, I see the grate over the drain in the middle of the tile floor begin to vibrate.

Grrrrrrrrrr, grrrrrrrrrr, grrrrrrrrrr... burp!

The grate lifts at one end, releasing a big turd that shoots across the floor, skidding to a stop next to the claw foot of the tub.

Not my turd, incidentally.

Water starts bubbling up behind it, covering the floor with a selection of our guests' leavings.

Good god, that is disgusting, and I speak as a mother familiar with infant bowel movements. I'll have to get Danny to bolt the drain to the floor to prevent any more fecal launches.

Scooping the offending waste into the toilet, I mentally draft the polite wording to make little signs above each sink. I can only imagine Prunella's reaction at having a poo launch itself at her from across the room.

Danny is already in the kitchen when I come down after my bath.

'Happy Christmas!' he says. He's wearing green and grey striped socks with his breeches.

'You're looking very festive.'

'Yeah, well these were the only other knee-length

socks I have.'

'I'm sorry I gave your others away.'

'Don't mention it. I can buy a new pair with the £1,000 you're paying me.'

I feel uncomfortable at the mention of the money.

Stop it, Lottie. It's simply a financial transaction. There's nothing to feel uncomfortable about. Even if I am starting to wish that money wasn't part of the equation.

'Look what the ladies left for us.' He lifts the edge of the tea towel covering an assortment of oddly shaped eggs. No two are the same.

'That's scrambled eggs for everyone then.'

'Speaking of which, what else is on the menu today?' he asks.

I can't tell if he's also ill at ease about last night.

'There's that beautiful beef in the fridge. I thought we could do that with potatoes and vegetables. And we've got the Christmas pudding for dessert. If we feed them enough we may not have to make peanut butter sandwiches again tonight. Should we make lunch a little later, say around four?'

'As long as the children won't have to wait until afterwards to open their presents. That's cruel and unusual punishment.'

But we don't need to fear for the twins' feelings. I can hear them both screaming blue murder as they run down the stairs. Of course Prunella and Hugo won't make them wait. That would require some actual parenting, and neither seems keen to fill that position.

Rupert appears not long after his niece and nephew.

'Happy Christmas, did you sleep well?' Danny asks.

'Until the banshees woke, yes, thanks. Happy

Christmas to you both. Is breakfast on the schedule this morning?'

'Absolutely!' I say. 'If you'd like to go in to the dining room, the table is set, so sit anywhere you'd like. I can bring in coffee or tea?'

'Coffee, please.'

'And would you like eggs? Beans? Bacon and toast?'

'Yes, I'll have two soft boiled eggs please.'

Somehow I just knew he'd say that.

Hugo and Prunella come into the dining room together just as I'm serving Rupert his breakfast. It seems to be the one meal that Danny does actually know how to cook. If only we can convince our guests that the Victorians ate only fry-ups.

I'm not sure why I'm so surprised by Hugo and Prunella's joint appearance. After all, they are married to each other. It's inevitable that their paths will cross occasionally, like two weather systems conspiring to make a cyclone.

'Beautiful day!' Hugo says, peering out the window at the bright blue sky. 'What's on the agenda before lunch?'

He looks at me.

Rupert looks at me.

Even Prunella deigns to look at me.

Is it my job to entertain them as well as to feed, bathe and rest them? 'I'm afraid I'm not really from around here, so...'

'There are a few nice walks that run close to the house,' Danny says as he brings in a pot of tea. He looks perfectly comfortable in the house now, like he lives here all the time.

'If you wanted to go for a walk after breakfast, I'll be happy to take you. It is a beautiful day. Lottie, would you like to come too?'

'Yes, Lottie, please do,' says Hugo.

'Oh no, thanks, you go ahead. I'll need to do some cleaning before lunch. Do take Mabel though, Danny, if you don't mind looking after her.'

'I don't mind at all. What do you say, Mabel? Do you want to come for a walk with us?'

She's just come into the dining room with Amanda and Oliver. All three are whispering together.

'Yes please!' Mabel says.

'What about you two?' Rupert asks. 'Do you fancy a little walk after breakfast?'

'I hate walks!' Amanda shouts. 'I won't go and you can't make me.'

'Walks are for losers,' Oliver adds, looking straight at his uncle. 'That makes you a loser.'

I bet Rupert is really sorry not to have sprung for that holiday to Tanzania.

'Well then you'll just have to stay here,' Prunella says. 'A walk will do me good. What time will we eat?'

'I'll just prepare everything before we go and we can eat around four,' Danny says.

'Make it two o'clock,' she says. 'I don't want to eat late.'

CHAPTER ELEVEN

What have I gotten myself into? I'm used to parenting a moderately challenging but essentially well-behaved child, not the spawn of Satan. Oliver and Amanda won't be easy to reason with, and if I lock them in their room they'll probably chew their way out.

'Well I'm sure you got some nice presents from Father Christmas,' although they deserve a lump of coal and smack on the arse. 'Why don't you play with those?'

'I'm bored!'

'Me too.'

'Great, then you can come upstairs with me and clean the bathrooms. Shall I get you some rubber gloves?'

They run together into the parlor.

Sometimes reverse psychology does work.

I go into Prunella's room first. It's a tip. There are towels strewn all over the bed and the duvet has been pulled on to the floor. I wonder if that's where she makes Hugo sleep, in a little nest at the foot of the bed.

One end of the rug is coated in talcum powder and

there are ring marks on the side tables where they haven't bothered to use the coasters. It's probably good that they usually go away for expensive holidays. At least then the hotel owners can use some of the money to fix what they've ruined during their stay.

I tidy up as best as I can, take a deep breath and move on to Rupert's room. Lord only knows what I'll find there.

But it doesn't even look like he's staying in the room. The bed is perfectly made. There isn't one personal item in sight. Does he levitate over the mattress, or sleep in the wardrobe, perhaps hanging upside down from the clothes rail?

The only clue that he's been there is that the bed is much more precisely made than I managed yesterday. Hats off to Rupert. He wins my vote for guest of the year.

The duvets are also pulled over the mattresses in the twins' room, but I know by their shoddy arrangement that Rupert wasn't the chambermaid here.

They may have the manners of the girls at St Trinian's but at least the twins tried to make their beds, as haphazard as the effort is.

Smiling to myself, I whip back the first duvet to straighten it.

That's when the odor hits me.

This is a cover-up. Literally.

I smell bed-wetters.

Mabel went through a short phase after my parents died where nightly accidents became an issue, but luckily she stopped as suddenly as she started and we haven't had to worry about it since.

I should be furious about Aunt Kate's wee-stained

mattresses, but my heart goes out to the twins. They didn't do it on purpose.

Unlike the cat.

I find their sodden pajamas balled up under one of the beds. I can wash and dry them and get them back to their room in time for bed, but the mattresses need cleaning.

After a lot of scrubbing, I'm just drying the second mattress with my hairdryer when I hear everyone coming back. They sound like they're in high spirits.

'Did you all have a good time?' I ask, watching Danny's expression for signs of a struggle.

'It was very nice,' he says. 'Look what Mabel found.'

She holds out a long feather. 'It's a peasant feather!'

'It's beautiful,' I say. 'I think you mean pheasant.'

She looks at Danny for confirmation. 'Pheasant,' she says. 'And we saw a live one too in the field.'

'I'm glad you had fun, but I'm glad you're back too. I missed you.' I hug her close.

'I'll just put lunch on,' Danny says.

'And how about some of that cocktail too?' Hugo asks. 'After all, it is a holiday, and nearly past noon. How were the children?'

'Oh, they were fine. I hardly even noticed them here,' I say.

'Where are they?'

I look around. That's a good question.

'They're off playing,' I say. 'Would you like a cup of tea to warm up? The parlor is toasty with the fire going.'

Once I get the adults safely into the parlor, I go looking for the children that I've carelessly misplaced.

'Oliver, Amanda!' I whisper.

Upstairs I check behind all the curtains and under the beds.

'Are you playing hide and seek?'

I look in each cabinet and closet.

'Where are you, you little brats?!'

I get back downstairs to the kitchen just in time to see Danny cutting up the last bit of beef.

'What are you doing?!'

There's a huge mound of cubed beef on the chopping board.

'Just getting the meat ready for the stew. What are you doing?'

'I'm trying to find those damn children. Do you realize you've just cut up a Chateaubriand?'

'Are you speaking English?'

'It's supposed to be cooked whole and sliced at the table for everyone. Not used for stewing beef.'

That meat cost me nearly sixty quid. I glare at him. 'You don't really know how to cook, do you?'

'I thought that would have been obvious yesterday.'

'Then why accept a job cooking?' I say, flinging open each of the cabinets, just in case there's a child wedged in there.

'You know why,' he mutters. 'And you would have done exactly the same thing.'

He's right. Of course he's right. If Mabel lived on the other side of the world, I'd do anything to see her.

'I'm sorry,' I say. 'It's not like I could cook any of these ingredients either. I've just eaten out at nice restaurants in London so I thought a few fancy meals would impress Rupert. I am really sorry.'

Suddenly it's very important for him to say it's okay, that he forgives me.

'Lottie, I live on fry-ups and takeaways. If it's not Chinese, Indian or fish and chips, I haven't had much experience with it. So I'm sorry. I should have told you I couldn't cook.'

'Do you really know how to make a stew, or was this another salmon-in-salmon Danny special?'

He flinches. 'I think Mum used to put a bunch of meat and veg into a pot of water and boil it for a few hours. That should work, right?'

'Like I would know! I've never even seen stew made, so you're ahead of me. While I go look for the twins, see if you can get a recipe off the internet.'

The twins aren't in the fridge either.

It's time to panic.

I return to the parlor where everyone is in the same position as yesterday. How quickly we find our routines, even when away.

'It is a lovely day,' I say, walking to each of the windows and pulling back the curtains.

No twins fall out.

'Would anyone like another board game? We have lots here.'

I fling open the cabinet at the side of the book shelves. No children.

'Hugo, see if the twins are hungry,' says Prunella. 'If they are the cook can make them lunch early.'

Hugo rises, draining his glass. 'Lottie, are the twins in the conservatory?'

'Um, they must be.'

I hurry after him.

Of course they'll be in the conservatory. It's the sunniest room in the house and it's probably where Mingus is trying to snatch some peace and quiet. Since he's making it his goal to leave his fur on all the soft furnishings he wouldn't want to miss out the sofas there.

I'm right about Mingus at least.

'Hmm, where are they? Lottie?'

I look all around, as if he's overlooked his own children.

'I'm afraid I don't exactly know.'

His eyes widen. 'You don't know? You don't know where my children are? They could be anywhere in the house?' His voice rises. 'Anywhere in the wood for that matter? Or playing beside the road? Prunella!' he bellows.

Rupert strides into the conservatory a minute later. 'Must you shout, Hugo? What is it?'

'She's lost the children.'

Rupert looks confused. 'Lost them?'

'I haven't exactly lost them, Rupert. I just don't have them to hand at this moment. I think they're hiding. They have to be here somewhere.'

That sends them both off shouting for Oliver and Amanda. Through every room they stomp, with me following meekly behind. By the time we get back to the parlor, I'm nearly as panicked as they are.

Prunella hasn't left the sofa. 'They must be here somewhere, Hugo. You know how they like to hide.'

'Prunella, you're worse than a cat when it comes to those children. Could you please at least try to care that your offspring have disappeared? God, they might have been snatched. Were all the doors locked?' he asks me.

'I- I don't-'

Mabel has been watching this exchange with interest.

'They're probably in the dungeon,' she says.

'What dungeon, sugarpea?'

'Downstairs. I don't like it down there. I think there are spiders.'

Her words send us all scrambling for the back stairs. We can hear the twins as soon as I open the door.

'Where's the light?!' Hugo asks. 'I'm coming, darlings, I'm coming!'

Amanda and Oliver rush through the coal cellar door as soon as I open it. Their faces are black with ancient coal dust except for teary streaks down their cheeks.

'We got locked in!' Amanda says, hugging her dad.

'It's pitch black in there, and cold,' adds Oliver. 'I thought the cat might be hiding in there.'

Rupert flicks the old-fashioned iron door latch up and down. 'You really should padlock it,' he says. 'It latches shut whenever the door is pulled closed.'

'I'm so sorry. I didn't think the children would go in there. I'll have Danny put a lock on it so it doesn't happen again. Oliver, Amanda, why don't we go upstairs by the fire so you can warm up? I'll draw your baths.'

The idea of bathing is clearly more upsetting than being locked in the coal cellar could ever be. Amanda's lip quivers.

'If you give me their clothes when they've changed,' I say to Hugo, 'I'll wash and dry them for you. Again, I really am sorry.'

I can feel Aunt Kate's rating slipping further from my grasp.

CHAPTER TWELVE

'The important thing is that you found them, Mummy,' Mabel says, snuggling closer on our bed. 'So you don't have to be upset any more. There was no harm done.'

I wish that were true. What reviewer in his right mind would award a good rating to a B&B who's locked his relatives in the coal cellar? He'll have to flunk us on health and safety grounds alone.

Once we got the twins in to their baths, I needed a few minutes to myself. I had just enough time for a minor breakdown before lunch.

Unfortunately Mabel caught me in the act.

I don't like her to see me upset. When Mum and Dad died I didn't have much choice. I broke down in floods of tears at the least provocation. After that experience I tended to prioritize my upsets. If it's not a matter of life or death I try very hard not to cry.

This isn't life or death, but it is Aunt Kate's livelihood.

'Everything will be fine, I'm sure.' I sniff and

straighten my dress. 'Shall we go downstairs and see if we can help Danny?'

'All right, but first I want to tell you something.'

'What is it?'

'I'm proud of you, Mummy. You've done your best and that's all we can hope for. If you've done your best then you should hold your head up high.'

Out of the mouths of babes… I've told her that countless times. It's so nice to have some good words thrown back at me for a change.

'Thank you. I'm proud of us all. Remember what the house looked like when we arrived? Now look at it. Aunt Kate will be proud of us too. We'll serve Rupert and his family their Christmas dinner and see them on their way tomorrow.'

'I'll be glad to see the back of them,' she says. 'They're eating us out of house and home.'

That's Celine's favorite expression. At least I'm not the only one on Mabel's greatest hits list.

I send her into the kitchen to see how Danny is getting on so that I can set the table for lunch. With a few pine boughs woven between the candles and the sparkling glasses and silverware, it looks quite festive by the time I'm finished. I just need the Christmas crackers.

There are about a hundred in the cabinet under the stairs in the hall, but I have to crawl in to get them.

'Do you need a hand?'

Hugo stands behind me, making me very aware that my head is in the cabinet and my arse is in the hall.

'No, I'm fine, thanks.'

'You look fine from here.'

I back out, shuffling the boxes of crackers as I go.

'How are Amanda and Oliver? Happy again?'

Reminding him that he's fathered two children with Prunella should dampen his lust.

'There's no long-term damage. Here, let me help you with those.' He takes the boxes from me.

Fine, whatever. 'Thanks. I'll just set the table and then we're nearly ready for...'

He stops in the middle of the hall.

'Is something wrong?'

I stop too.

He shifts the boxes to one hand and points at the ceiling. 'Happy Christmas,' he says.

You've got to be kidding me. We're standing under the mistletoe that Danny hung to add a festive finishing touch for our guests' first impression. Clearly it's made an impression on Hugo.

'I have to finish laying the table,' I say. 'I'll take those. Thanks.'

And I'll get Danny to take the mistletoe down too. If I had a ladder I'd snatch it from the ceiling there and then.

The beef stew actually smells delicious. It might not win Danny any culinary awards for presentation, and is maybe an odd choice for Christmas lunch, but at least we've got something to serve Rupert.

They've downed a pitcher of cocktails by the time they pull their Christmas crackers. Maybe keeping the guests drunk is the way to garner positive reviews.

I'm standing slumped against the fridge watching Danny microwave the Christmas pudding.

'Are you sure it's all right to do that?' I ask.

'There isn't much choice. It would need to steam for

an hour and I forgot to start it before we served lunch. Besides, I looked it up on Google.'

'My Mum never microwaved it.'

'That's because Celine did the cooking, right?'

'You don't have to be mean about it, you know.'

His eyebrows shoot up. 'I wasn't trying to be mean. Didn't Celine do the cooking? That's what you told me.'

'Mum also cooked.'

'Then I stand corrected. I'm sorry… why are you so sensitive when I mention Celine?'

'I'm not,' I say, sensitively. 'I just don't need anyone judging me, that's all.'

'The last thing I'd do is judge you, Lottie. Come on. You're a single mum who's had a pretty shitty couple of years. If anything I'm jealous that you have Celine. And I admire you.'

The blush creeps up my cheeks. He admires me!

'Thanks, Danny. You're pretty admirable yourself, you know, the way you're devoted to your daughter. A lot of men don't bother.'

'I'm sorry about Mabel's father, Lottie, but not all men are shitbags. I hope you do know that.'

'Well I haven't had much exposure to men, shitbags or otherwise, since Mabel was born, so I'll have to take your word for it.'

Danny is beginning to restore my confidence though. If I were Phoebe's mother, I wouldn't have moved away.

The microwave pings and the moment passes.

I grab the brandy bottle and follow Danny to the dining room for our grand finale.

'Is everyone ready?' I say, holding the match over

the booze-soaked pudding. I always loved this part of Christmas lunch when Dad would set our pudding alight, sending mum into a fit of giggles every time.

I touch the match to the top of the pudding and it whooshes into blue flames that race down the sides.

Then they race around the plate.

Then they begin racing across the linen tablecloth, following the trail of brandy I've accidentally sloshed there.

'Look, Mummy, it's like bonfire night,' says Amanda, remarkably calm for someone witnessing a house fire.

It takes only seconds for the flames to take hold.

'Get some water!' Hugo shouts, pulling his family away from the table.

I dash to the kitchen for a pot of water, but by the time I get back, Danny is already there, pulling the pin on the fire extinguisher.

'I don't think we need—'

But it's too late. He aims the nozzle and shoots a white cloud of retardant all over Christmas lunch.

The fire is out. As is any possibility of pudding.

'We'll just go into the parlor,' Rupert says. 'Maybe we'll have our coffee in there?'

On the plus side, at least we don't need to worry about keeping everyone out of the dining room when the 8.30 train passes.

'I guess I overreacted,' Danny says, tucking his mobile phone away. He was talking to his daughter when I came upon him in the conservatory. I was embarrassed to catch him in such an intimate conversation, but his tone was so tender that I thought once again what a lucky little girl she is.

'Better safe than sorry, I guess. Aunt Kate wouldn't thank us if we burned her house down.'

He laughs. 'This has been the Fawlty Towers of Christmases. But it could have been worse.'

I raise my eyebrow. 'Not much worse.'

'Well at least we tried, and you can't do more than that.' He glances at my surprised expression. 'Sorry, I was being a dad. It's just something I say to Phoebe.'

'I say it to Mabel, too.'

For a moment we look at each other, possibly recognizing our common bond as single parents. And maybe, I dare to hope, maybe just a little bit more.

'You'll want a ride over to the hospital,' he says. 'I'll drive you.'

And suddenly I'm just his employer again.

There's a lot of activity around Aunt Kate's bed when we arrive. Two nurses are there with Doctor Londergan. My heartbeat quickens. Something is wrong.

'Doctor Londergan, what's happening?'

When she smiles, relief washes over me. It's good news.

'We discontinued the medication this afternoon and your aunt is coming around. We're just assessing her to make sure she's able to follow commands. Everything looks good.'

'Is she awake enough to know that we're here?'

'Why don't you ask her yourself?' she says, putting Aunt Kate's chart back into the slot at the end of her bed. 'We're finished now, so we can leave you in peace. Happy Christmas!'

'Thank you for everything you've done.' I pull her into a hug.

'It's my pleasure,' she says. 'I love a happy ending.'

Mabel and I bring the two grey plastic chairs close to Aunt Kate's bed. Maybe it's because she's sleeping instead of comatose, or because she no longer has the breathing mask over her face, or maybe it's my imagination now that I know the drugs have been stopped, but she looks different, better and more alive.

'Aunt Kate? It's Lottie.'

'And Mabel.'

'Today's Christmas Day, Aunt Kate, and the doctor says you're doing really well. That's the best gift in the world for us. Things are still fine at the B&B. Everyone had a nice dinner.'

There's no need to mention the need for the Fire Brigade.

'And Danny took them for a walk earlier. I think they've had a nice time.'

Best to keep the coal cellar incident quiet too.

'They'll leave early tomorrow morning and we can get back to normal and start looking forward to when you can come home.'

There's a bit of gloom on the horizon too though. It's not just the reviewer who'll leave tomorrow. Danny has honored our arrangement. Tomorrow he'll fulfil his promise and I'll have no reason to see him again.

'Can you hear me, Aunt Kate?'

'Her eyelids moved, Mummy! Did you see?'

'I did see!'

I feel my eyes fill with tears. Aunt Kate really is coming back to us.

CHAPTER THIRTEEN

Everyone is up early on Boxing Day, getting ready to make their escape back to London after breakfast. Danny's handiwork on the drains ensured there were no more smelly plumbing surprises and I even dare to hope the guests might get away without further incident.

The twins had one more go at the parlor, pulling everything off the shelves before Hugo got them strapped into the car. They'll probably grow into decent adults but, to quote Mabel quoting me, I'm definitely glad to see the back of them.

'So,' I say to Rupert as he hands me his room key. 'I do hope you enjoyed your stay with us. I'm sorry that there were a few... difficulties but I hope that won't affect Aunt Kate's rating.'

He knows I'm being cheeky but I've got nothing left to lose.

'It was an interesting visit. Please do thank your aunt for inviting us. I'll be submitting my review in early January when I'm back from holiday.'

'Oh, are you going somewhere nice for New Year's?'

He nods. 'I'm flying to Tanzania tomorrow. Alone.'

I smile. 'I understand completely. It's not always easy having family around.'

'Some families are easier than others. Most families are easier than mine.'

True as that is, I get the feeling I'm not supposed to agree with him. 'So, the rating then… could you give me a hint about how it went?'

He peers over the pile of cases he's trying to wedge into the overfilled boot. 'Well, I wasn't fooled by your Victorian theme. It was pretty clear you were bluffing by the time the peanut butter sandwiches came out, but I liked that you carried on with the theme in the face of complete implausibility. You're clearly very good at handling difficult guests. Frankly I'd have kicked Hugo in the bollocks and gone straight to my sister, so you showed remarkable restraint.'

He wouldn't think so if he knew I'd bitten his brother-in-law.

'The food was interesting…' he continues.

'It didn't turn out quite like I'd imagined.'

'Locking the children in the coal cellar when you were meant to be minding them certainly wasn't clever.'

I can only nod in agreement. I feel like the worst innkeeper in Britain. Maybe there's a rating for that. Given how hard I worked to honor the title, I may as well win something.

'And I've never seen a host set their dining table on fire before.'

The twins did think that was pretty cool though, so we should get some points for entertainment.

'But at the end of the day I came here to assess the B&B, which your aunt owns and runs. Presumably she runs it better than you.'

Ouch.

'It's definitely not perfect and she needs to sort out her plumbing before the health inspectors shut her down. As a B&B this is a reasonable business and does meet enough of our standards to warrant the rating.'

'Really?! That's wonderful, thank you so much!' I launch myself on Rupert.

'Ehem, yes, well, you're welcome.'

'Phew. I didn't think you were going to give it to us.'

The tiniest of smiles plays around his lips. 'Prunella doesn't like to admit it but our Granny's house looked a lot like this. It was draughty and a bit run down but the weekends I spent there as a child, lying in front of the fire in the parlor and eating Granny's cakes each teatime are some of my happiest memories. Your aunt has a special place here.' He brushes himself off and clears his throat. 'And as I said, most of the faults were because of you, not the B&B per se... You're not thinking of staying on to run it, are you?'

I shake my head. 'No, I'll go back to software programming where I belong.'

'That's best for all concerned.'

Mabel, Danny and I wave them off just before noon.

'That's that then,' says Danny as they pull out of sight.

Yes, it is, unless I do something fast.

'Do you know, I could use help taking down some of the decorations. I can't reach them without the ladder and don't want to climb up without someone holding it. Could you spare another half hour or so?'

I know I'm being ridiculous, playing the helpless

female to draw out my time with Danny. My inner feminist is hanging her head in shame. I just don't want to see him go yet.

He wrestles the ladder in from outside and sets it up against the first window in the hall. 'Do you want to climb up or hold the ladder?'

'I'd better climb,' I say. 'I'm not sure I could catch you if you fell off.'

'You've got a lot of faith in me.'

I pluck the pine boughs from the top of the valance and drop them on the floor. 'We got the rating you know.'

'You are joking!' he says. 'What were his criteria? Missing persons and pyrotechnics?'

I climb down and let him carry the ladder to the next window. Then I pull down more boughs, smiling as the pine scent washes over me.

'He said he appreciated our efforts,' I tell him. 'Even though he didn't buy the Victorian theme.'

'That reminds me. I never did get my socks back.'

'Sorry about that. I noticed Hugo packing them in the car and didn't think that was the time to tell him his children's Christmas stockings had come off your feet.'

We move to the last window.

'They were such a weird family,' he says.

He doesn't know the half of it. 'Rupert is going to Tanzania tomorrow, alone.'

'I don't blame him. I'd rather take my chances out in the bush with lions than spend any more time with Prunella.'

The last of the boughs hits the floor. 'That's all of them.'

I climb down.

'What about the mistletoe?'

It hangs there in the middle of the hall, an unwanted reminder of Hugo's attentions.

Danny positions the ladder beneath it, and puts his hands on either side of me so that I can climb up.

'Lottie? Wait a minute. There's something I-'

As I turn to face him, his warm lips meet mine. They're so perfectly soft but a little bit urgent that I know I want to stay in exactly this position for a very long time.

'Well we must have done something right,' he murmurs as we break off our kiss.

'Maybe they just loved your food.'

'Very funny.'

'No really, it wasn't bad. Although I wouldn't bother buying you expensive ingredients again.'

'Next time you can cook your own food.'

'I think we've established that I can't do that.'

'Then for both our sakes, I'd better take you out to dinner.'

We kiss again under the mistletoe.

Danny drives us to the hospital that afternoon as usual. But instead of sitting in the back seat, I sit up front so I can hold his hand between gear changes. Every time I look in the rear view mirror I catch Mabel's grin.

'We'll be two hours,' I tell Danny.

'Okay, I'll run home quickly, but I'll be here waiting when you get out.'

'Just like you were the first day.'

He smiles and kisses me again. 'Some things are worth waiting for.'

'Danny, there'll be plenty of time for that later,'

Mabel says. 'Right now we need to see Aunt Kate.'

I shrug. 'She's seven going on seventeen.'

'She's her mother's daughter. See you soon.'

'Aunt Kate, you're awake!' Mabel says when we get to her room. 'We've got so much to tell you!'

'Hello, love.' She pats the mattress beside her.

'Careful, Mabel,' I warn. 'How are you feeling?' I take my aunt's hand.

'I feel like I've been run down by a lorry, but it's better than the alternative. I gather I've been sleeping for a while.'

'Five days. The doctor has been great.'

She nods. 'She must have figured there's some life left in these old bones yet.'

'Mummy has a boyfriend,' Mabel says.

Aunt Kate peers at me. 'Does she now?'

Mabel nods. 'His name is Danny and he's our cook but not really our cook. He's also our taxi driver. But not really that either. He's really our friend. That's right, isn't it, Mummy?'

'That's right. There's a lot to tell you, Aunt Kate, but most importantly, the reviewer loved the B&B and he's going to give you the rating you need.'

'Oh that is wonderful news! So everything went well then?'

'Except for the fire,' says Mabel.

'Like I said, there's a lot to tell you. Are you tired though? We can always talk more tomorrow.'

'Don't you dare leave, Lottie. I want to hear every detail. Especially about this boyfriend of yours.'

Aunt Kate is mightily impressed with our ingenuity at the B&B. I try glossing over some of the gorier details but Mabel is a stickler for the whole truth, not to mention a very observant little girl who seemed to know that Danny and I liked each other before we realized it ourselves.

'I'm just sorry that I've missed Christmas,' Aunt Kate says. 'I do so love Christmas.'

'You haven't missed it. We're staying here until you get out, and then we'll all have Christmas together.'

'Will you really?'

I nod. 'I'm not going to go back to London just yet. You'll need help while your leg is healing, and I can work remotely for a few weeks. Mabel doesn't have to be back in school until mid-January.'

'That will be wonderful, Lottie,' Aunt Kate says. 'It's all quite wonderful, really.'

As promised, Danny is waiting for us when we leave the hospital.

'Aunt Kate's awake!' Mabel says. 'And we get to stay in Wales to have another Christmas. Does that mean we get more presents from Father Christmas, Mummy?'

'No, honey, I'm afraid he doesn't do encore performances. You'll have to wait till next year, but remember you've still got lots of gifts at home.'

'You are staying here for a while?' Danny asks, grabbing my hand.

'For at least a few weeks,' I say.

'I fly to the US tomorrow, but I'll be back in a week.'

'And then…'

'And then we'll work something out,' he says. 'It's not ideal with me here and you in London, but it is only a few hours by train. I could come down and, if you don't mind traveling a bit, you and Mabel could come here too?'

We kiss again. I can't seem to get enough of him. 'I don't mind at all. What do you say, Mabel? Would you like to spend more weekends at Aunt Kate's?'

'Definitely, Mummy. Now that Mingus and I are friends, he'd be sad if we don't see each other. And Aunt Kate still needs to make me her Welsh cakes. I could murder one of those.'

'I'll tell you what, Mabel,' says Danny. 'I'll look up a recipe on the internet and make you some when we get back.'

We both stare at him.

'That's okay, Danny,' Mabel says, patting his shoulder. 'We'd better wait for Aunt Kate to make them.'

The End

Every time you write a review, an author gets a cupcake, so if you enjoyed *The Reluctant Elf*, please take a minute to share your thoughts on your favorite book websites.

ABOUT THE AUTHOR

Michele Gorman is the USA TODAY and Sunday Times bestselling author of eight romantic comedies. Born and raised in the US, Michele has lived in London for 17 years. She is very fond of naps, ice cream and Richard Curtis films but objects to spiders and the word "portion".

You can find out more about Michele by following her Twitter or Facebook. Do chat with her on twitter or Facebook – she's always looking for an excuse to procrastinate!

@MicheleGormanUK

Michele Gorman Books

The Curvy Girls Club

Where Confidence is the New Black

Fed up with always struggling to lose weight, best friends Katie, Ellie, Pixie and Jane start a social club where size doesn't matter. It soon grows into London's most popular club - a place to have fun instead of counting carbs - and the women find their lives changing in ways they never imagined.

But outside the club, life isn't as rosy.

"This is a delightful book of friendship, acceptance, and belonging for anyone who has ever wondered: "What if?"" *Publishers Weekly*

Perfect Girl

Cinderella *meets* Falling Down *in this wickedly funny tale about having it all*

Carol is perfect... at least that's what everyone thinks. In reality she's sinking fast – her family treats her like their personal assistant and her boyfriend is so busy with work that he's got her single-handedly running their relationship. Not that her job is any easier. As the only woman on the bank's trading floor she spends twelve-hour days trying not to get sworn at or felt up by colleagues who put the "W" in banker.

How long can she go on pleasing everyone else before she snaps and loses it all?

With humor and empathy, Perfect Girl lays bare the balancing act that working women face in a man's world

Read on for an excerpt of **Perfect Girl**

Perfect Girl
PART ONE
Chapter 1.

The flashes start as soon as I stumble through the revolving door. Ping, ping, ping. Little white boxes burning across my vision.

'Look here! Hey, this way! Darlin', over here!'

Someone tipped off the media. I could turn away, try to hide my face like the A-listers do, but that'd seem a bit pretentious for someone so far down the popularity alphabet. There are at least a dozen photographers flanking us. I'll have to go down the steps. Even if there was another way out, they'd probably find it. I'm surprised so many are bothering with us. This isn't Boujis and I'm not exactly with Prince Harry.

We're attracting quite a bit of attention now. More and more people are holding their phones up, trying to snatch something worth tweeting. They have no idea who we are. They're just hoping to capture the photo that'll catapult them towards viral Instagram fame.

At least I got to touch up my lipstick before we left. There's nothing worse than those unguarded photos of a woman tumbling from a nightclub with the smudged smile of a psychotic clown. Well, okay, of course there's worse, but I am wearing knickers and my skirt's not too short.

I can see the car now. It's ticking over beside the curb in a double red zone. Rock Star parking.

As he opens the passenger door (courteous to the

end) I think about how far I've come. I can even point to where it started, with Dad's party. Has my life really changed so completely in six months? Time sure does fly.

'Mind your head,' he says as he gently pushes me into the police car. He joins the other Met officer in front as the reporters aim their cameras into the windows and howl like a pack of overexcited hounds.

'Why did you do it, Carol?'

'Are you sorry?'

Over and over they repeat their questions, like there's a simple answer.

At least they don't turn on the lights as we pull away. After all, there's no need to rush now.

Chapter 2.

Six months earlier…

I feel Ben's lanky body slip into bed behind me. My first thought is, *He's drunk*. My second thought, when he pulls me to him is, *Suck in your tummy*.

Urgh, too late. Palm full of squidge for my boyfriend. It's his own fault, really. He needs fitting with a bell to give me some warning, like Mum did with the cat to stop him killing sparrows in the garden.

'What time is it?' I murmur. Last year the sleep clinic made me take the clock out of my bedroom. Now I just get up to check the one in the kitchen, adding insult to insomnia.

'It's after two, I'm sorry.' He snuggles closer, reeking of gin. I hate gin, but I love him, so things kind of balance out. 'I probably should have called first, but I didn't want to wake you. You did say I could let myself in any time, right?'

True. When I gave him the newly-cut key tied with pink ribbon six months ago I imagined my bed strewn with rose petals, surprise dinners, my flat redecorated by the *Changing Rooms* team, obvious things like that. He's used it once to let the boiler man in when I couldn't get away from the office.

'You went for a drink after?' Question, not accusation.

'Yeah. We grabbed something for dinner and ended up staying out.' He hesitates. 'I'll have to go back in tomorrow.'

I fizz awake. 'But it's Dad's birthday party tomorrow.'

'I know, I'm sorry,' he says to the back of my head, his face buried in my sheet-frazzled hair. 'You know we're preparing for court. I can't work without the others there. It's a team project.' He grabs my tummy again. This time I'm ready for him. 'I wanted to see you tonight.'

'It's not tonight. It's tomorrow.'

'I wanted to see you tomorrow, too.'

… 'I'm tired, Ben.'

'No ulterior motives, I promise. At least not till I get some sleep first.'

I smile in the dark. 'I'm glad you came over. Though I wish you could come to Dad's tomorrow.'

'Me too. You know I would if I could. I don't want to spend my Sunday working.'

'I know,' I say, pulling his arm around me to hold his hand. 'Like Mum always says, it's the price you pay for your success.'

Lately, though, it's felt like *my* purse being emptied.

* * * * *

My parents' house is bright enough to lure migrating birds off course. In the weak winter twilight, gold and purple metallic bunting reflects flashing strings of fairy lights. Lilac balloons decorate the posts beside the drive and a twenty-foot long banner (*Happy 55th Joel!*) is stretched across the windows at the front. If Dad had his way, he'd hide in his studio till the whole thing blows over. If Mum has hers, we'll be the lead story on

The One Show.

I stagger towards the front door, still grizzling about my sister's phone call.

'Just a few things to pick up for me, will you please?' Marley had said. 'I'm running late. Have you got a pen?'

Half a dozen Tesco bags rub against my knees. A bargain pack of coat hangers pokes through the flimsy plastic, hitching up the side of my new dress and threatening to run my tights.

The familiar wall of warmth envelops me when I step into the front hall. My parents aren't what you'd call 'jumper people'. For them the perfect ambient temperature hovers around that of the Sahara at midday.

Despite the stress of the past few months, it's good to be home again, even if my eyes are beginning to desiccate.

'Hello, darling!' Mum says as she hugs me. I can hear everyone laughing in the living room. Our neighbors like to hit the bottle early. Mrs. McConnell will be Irish step dancing by the time Dad blows out his birthday candles.

'What took you so long? Did you get caught up in traffic?'

Mum steps back, appraising the deep blue jersey dress and matching suede platform heels I bought for today. Satisfied, she tucks a lock of my thick blonde hair behind my ear. She's always doing that because, she says, I've got too much hair for my face. 'You look lovely, but you've laddered your tights.'

I don't bother saying that this is Marley's fault.

'Where's Dad's cake?' she asks.

'I've only got two hands.' I shift my BlackBerry and

keys back to my handbag. 'It's in the car, and I'm late because I had to pick up some things that Marley needed. She should be here soon.'

'She's been here for ages! She's in the kitchen.'

'Then I'm so glad I was able to take the stress out of her day.'

'Stop being dramatic. You needed to go to the shop anyway.' She peers over my shoulder. 'Where's Ben?'

'Working. He sends his love, but he'll probably be at the office till late. They're still preparing for that case.'

She nods. Work excuses are the norm in our family. Marley works at the same bank as me, though in another department in a different building. As the investment banking boss's secretary her hours are more regular than mine but she does sometimes get caught up in important meetings (all meetings are important to bankers). And Dad's schedule has always been haphazard.

'Drop the bags upstairs, please, and go get the cake,' Mum says. 'We're all dying to see it.' Her face is flushed with excitement, or possibly heat stroke. Either way, she's beautiful. Tall and regal, her pencil skirt and crisp white blouse accentuates the slim waist she proudly maintains despite having had two children, and her deep auburn updo shows off the diamond and pearl earrings that Dad got her for their thirtieth wedding anniversary last year. My mum, the red-hot stunner of Netherhaven Close.

Upstairs, I can hear the sound of running water coming from the bathroom. The lights are on; the tap is going full-throttle and a half-eaten marmalade sandwich balances on the edge of the bath.

Zoe.

Her room is empty but when I shove open the guest bedroom door it flies closed again with a painful thud. 'Don't come in!' shouts Zoe. 'I'm dressing! Undressing. I'm undressing!'

'Zoe, it's me, open up. Why are you undressing in the guest room?' Carefully, I open the door again. 'You left the tap running in the bathroom.'

'Did I?' she asks vaguely and, I note, fully dressed. 'I was having a sandwich.'

As if that explains the tap. She moves to the window seat in the dark. A lighter flares.

It takes a moment for my eyes to adjust. 'Are you smoking pot?' I say as I flick on the light.

'Turn that off! Don't tell Madame Colbert.'

'As if I would.' I flip the switch. 'When did you develop a drug habit?'

'It is not a drug habit,' she scoffs, making me feel like her grandmother. 'It is no worse than you having a glass of wine.'

'Except that my glass of wine is legal.'

I may as well wag a finger at her and peer over bifocals. Old woman.

'Don't be such a geek. I have only just tried it. I am still deciding if it suits me.'

When she speaks like this it's hard to remember that when Mum and Dad sent away for their very own foreign student, she wasn't yet completely fluent in English. She came from a village near Toulouse for a three-month stint, charmingly dropped all her h's and made us fall hopelessly in love with her. She's pretty much lived in my old bedroom for the past six years. She goes back to France each year around Christmas, where she gets reacquainted with the family that raised her. Then she returns to England to the family that thinks of her as one of our own.

She turns to blow another stream of smoke, the bulbs outside backlighting her long, dark, candy floss hair, which she likes to pin in a pile atop her head. 'You will not tell?' She sounds much younger than her twenty-one years.

My hug dislodges the sweetly pungent aroma from her grey velvet dress, which Mum will say is too depressing for a party. 'Of course not. But you smell like an Amsterdam coffee shop. Here.' I rummage in my handbag for the little vial of perfume I keep for office emergencies. 'And you'd better clean your teeth before you go downstairs. You know what Mum will say if she thinks you've been smoking. It's bad enough that I do it.'

'Yes, and speaking of that, you should not have your gum.'

I completely forgot to get rid of the Nicorette in the car.

'Do you know you are buzzing?' she asks.

I snatch my BlackBerry from my bag to scroll through the new emails. Just a dozen or so. Not bad for a Sunday.

As Zoe rises from the window seat I say, 'Why aren't you in your own room?'

'It is too close to the stairs. Madame Colbert might smell something.' She appraises me. 'That doesn't occur to you, I suppose.' She shakes her head. 'I wonder if you have ever done anything wrong in your life.'

I blush at the compliment, then realize as I jog down the stairs to retrieve Dad's cake from the car that she probably means to be insulting.

But she's right. For twenty-six years running in our family drama (now celebrating its thirty-first spectacular year in Greater London), I have reprised the role of The Good Daughter. It's a character I work hard to perfect, and one that means everything to me. My family's compliments are the tokens that top up my self-esteem. I guess most people are the same.

In the kitchen, Mum and Marley are busy piling M&S canapés on to enormous golden serving trays for the waiters I've hired for the day. Granny supervises from her wheelchair. 'Hello, doll,' she says as I kiss her powdery cheek. 'You look gorgeous!'

She always says this, but that's Granny for you. She came to live with us just after I started secondary school. Mum was worried about her being on her own after Granddad died, and didn't trust my Auntie Lou to look after her. I don't blame her. Auntie Lou means well but she can hardly look after her house plants.

Dad had the garage converted into a flat for Granny, all on one level, with a ramp to get into the house through the back. So Marley and I got to grow up with our Granny within wheeling distance.

'Here's the cake!' I announce, opening the bakery box so Granny can see. 'What do you think? Isn't it beautiful?'

'Wow, well done!' Marley says, clapping her manicured hands. 'Jez!' she calls into the hallway when she spots her boyfriend. 'Come and see the cake.'

He ambles in, kissing me hello.

Mum was thrilled when Marley produced Jez for our inspection. She was glad to see my sister finally putting her Cambridge education to good use.

It's a sore subject round the dinner table. Mum thinks being a secretary (even a great one like Marley) is beneath her. A lawyer, doctor or rocket scientist would be more in keeping with our status as the as-yet-undiscovered heirs to the Romanoff dynasty.

But Jez's architect credentials trump even my banking job in the bragging stakes (well-paid and creative). He's every mother's dream and she nearly adopted him when she learned that his great uncle had been knighted. Jez told me that this uncle was a sociopath, avoided by the family, but we let Mum enjoy the fact that she's one degree of separation from a Sir.

'Wow, that looks incredible,' says Jez, admiring the cake. 'Can I have a slice?'

Marley shoves him away. 'Not till we sing to Dad! Go, get out. Go talk to Ben.'

Instead, he takes her hand and kisses her. Unlike the rest of us, Jez doesn't always let Marley get her way.

'Ben's not coming,' I tell them. 'He's got to work.'

'Oh, that's a shame!' Marley says, searching my expression with sisterly vigilance for any sign of upset. I keep my smile bright.

'You've done well, Carol,' says Mum, running her expert eye over the confection. 'This is perfect.'

I'm grinning like an idiot. When Mum told me what she wanted I never imagined finding someone to make it. But after visiting nearly every baker within the M25 to sample their offerings, it was worth it (even the squidgy tummy). As far as show-stoppers go it's even better than the 1920s chocolate fountain that I sourced for Marley's birthday party a few years ago. It might even top Mum and Dad's anniversary entertainment, at least in impact if not effort. You'd have thought I was commissioning Spielberg to direct a feature film about them, not just asking someone to write, direct and shoot a Super 8 film commemorating their thirty years together, with a few interviews of their friends and family and an on-location shoot in Australia where they met.

'I thought you were running late, Marley,' I remind her as I help with the last of the canapés. 'Something about being too stressed to do your own shopping?' She looks about as stressed as our cat after his nap. 'I put the bags in the spare bedroom, by the way. You owe me seventy-five quid.'

'Thanks, you are a star,' she says, digging the money out of her handbag. Marley always keeps a wad of cash to hand, and only uses her cards for important things like shoe investments. Her closets are drool-worthy but she's not a spendthrift. Groomed by our mother, we are women who dress for our success.

'I was running late,' she says. 'That's why I didn't have time to do the shopping. Did you have them use margarine instead of butter in the cake?'

I shake my head, puzzled. Marley's not one to worry about nutrition. She's been blessed with Mum's figure, despite having Dad's appetite. I try not to hate her for her genetic Lotto jackpot.

'Oh, well, it's not really important.'

She purses her lips.

'It's just that margarine would have been a bit healthier for everyone. You know, since Dad's agent had that heart attack. Never mind. I'm sure a slice of cake won't kill him.'

'It's that twenty years of alcoholism that'll kill him,' Granny says, tactful as always. She drives Mum nuts with these outbursts but the doctors say she's not got dementia. Marley and I think she's marvelous.

'Should I run out for some light ice cream at least?'

I've bought enough of the full-fat stuff to send the entire neighborhood to the emergency room.

'You are going for ice cream?' Zoe says, drifting in on a cloud of my perfume. 'I would like a bowl.' She opens the fridge. 'Will you get me the one I like, with the marshmallows and chocolate?'

'Nobody's going for ice cream,' Mum says. 'Now that we're all here, I want everyone in the sitting room talking to our guests. No hiding in the kitchen like you usually do. Marley, be sure to tell Mrs. Latham about your promotion. She was bragging about her son the other day and she cut me off before I could tell her your good news. And Carol, Mr. Templeton was asking about you. I'm sure he'd love to know how well you're doing at the bank.'

Our mum holds an Olympic gold medal in bragging. An entire wall in the kitchen is devoted to our awards, from Marley's first Practicing Certificate to my Duke of Edinburgh Silver Award. Even worse, she actually shows them to people, like our neighbors will be impressed by my Fire Safety badge.

'And Zoe…' Mum appraises her. 'I do wish you wouldn't always look like you've dressed for a funeral.'

'Madame Colbert, this is trendy,' Zoe says, wandering toward the granite-topped island where the cake sits. 'Oh, très jolie!'

The bakers have captured Dad's garden perfectly, right down to the tiny shovel and clippers lying beside his beloved weather-worn shed. His creaky old wheelbarrow spills over with sugar paste tulips and hyacinths, set upon the path through rose bushes and flowering beds. It looks almost too good to eat. Almost.

Marley wanted us to do a guitar cake to commemorate Dad's career, but Mum was right. The garden is his oasis away from the madness, and a much more fitting way to mark his birthday.

'I think Zoe looks lovely,' I say, slapping her hand as she plays amateur gardener by sticking her finger into the grass. Her heart-shaped face and wide eyes make her look like a naughty pixie.

'What's that smell?' Mum asks, sniffing.

I quickly shuffle closer to Zoe. 'Oh, I'm afraid that's me, Mum. I spilled a bit of perfume on my dress. Sorry, it should air out in a little while.'

Mum puts her hand to her temple. 'Maybe you could borrow one of Zoe's dresses, darling. It really is too strong.'

I nod. 'It's giving me a bit of a headache, too. Come on, Zoe, I need to look in your closet.'

'Hmm? You can help yourself, you know where everything is,' she says, still eying the cake, her Class B offense completely forgotten.

'Come on, Zoe. I need your help.' I've got to get her back upstairs before Mum realizes that she's the stinky one. 'You need to change,' I tell her, sighing as we mount the stairs. 'And thanks to you, now so do I.'

Dad settles gratefully into his favorite chair after the last of our neighbors stagger home to sleep off the kick of our Moscow Mule recipe. Mom's buzzing with success, having impressed everyone with her offspring's latest feats. And the caterers are clearing up, leaving us wracked with middle-class guilt and at a loose end. We sit in the living room trying not to make eye contact with our servers.

'We have an announcement,' Marley says as Jez grabs her hand. 'As you know, we went away to the country last weekend for our anniversary. Our fifth. What's the gift for a fifth anniversary?'

'It's silverware,' Jez says, smiling.

'And that's appropriate since silver is made into what?' She pauses, possibly just to torture Mum who, I can see, is dying to shout out the punch line. 'Jewelry. And while we were there, Jez proposed. We're getting married!'

Our squeals unsettle the caterers as we rush to hug the nearly-weds, everyone talking at once. Finally, Marley raises her hand when Mum asks if Jez's great uncle will be invited.

'Give us a chance, we've only been engaged a few days! We haven't worked out all the details yet. All we know is that we want a winter wedding. And that we'd love for Carol to be our bridesmaid.'

She takes my hands, with Jez grinning behind her. 'Will you, Carol? Will you be my bridesmaid?'

My eyes well up. I've loved Jez, with or without his sociopathic family member, from the day we met. To think that with all the friends Marley has, she's chosen me!

'Of course I will, thank you. Of course!'

'Fantastic.' She kisses me. 'This is going to be such fun. There are a million things to take care of but I know we can rely on you completely. You did such an incredible job with the party, didn't she, Dad?'

Dad stands up and catches me up in a bear hug as

Mum looks on. 'I should have known this was all down to you, Carol. Thank you, my darling girl. I'm sure you did so much beyond what I've even noticed today. You always do. This has been a wonderful day, and it's all thanks to you.'

'Oh, well. We all helped, really. But thank you.'

Dad knows that's a lie but he also knows I don't want the attention on myself. I like my approval whispered in my ear, not shouted for everyone to hear. I'd have made an excellent behind-the-scenes theatre type, maybe the guy who does the lights or writes the music. Then I could sit hidden in the wings reveling in the audience's applause.

'Anyway,' Marley continues, drawing everyone back to her news. Unlike me, she suffers no sensitivity to limelight. 'We've been thinking about churches. Someplace tiny and ancient, in a quaint little village, but with excellent transport links, and of course it has to be close to the reception venue. Wouldn't a stately home be perfect? Maybe you can find one that doesn't charge an arm and a leg. And my dress. We can all go shopping together, but we'll need to make appointments quickly to have time for the fittings. We have to choose rings, and the cake, hotels for the guests. Oh, it's crazy to think we can pull it all together in just a year, but I know you can do it!'

'Of course,' I say weakly, realizing what this means for my already meagre allotment of free time. 'Maybe Zoe can help me, since she's not working yet.'

'But I might not be around,' Zoe says, tucking in to another great wodge of cake.

'When might you not be around?' Marley asks.

'When's the wedding?'

'Winter!' Mom and Marley say, trading looks.

'Zoe should concentrate on finding a job,' Mum says. 'It's been nearly a year now.'

'But I've been writing.'

Marley rolls her eyes. 'Poems won't pay your rent.'

I don't want to hear this argument again.

'But I don't need to pay my rent,' Zoe says.

'That's the whole point,' Marley shoots back. 'You live with Mum and Dad!'

Zoe looks baffled by this statement. I hate when they pick on her like this. If she were a deer, she'd have a giant bull's-eye painted on her side during hunting season.

Marley's objection isn't really about Zoe's employment status, although that does wind her up hilariously. Zoe's parents send a check each month to cover her living expenses, and seem happy to do so until she draws a pension.

Marley doesn't think Zoe is particularly smart. She's wrong, though. Dimwits don't become fluent in English in six years. She's possibly just better suited to eighteenth-century novels than boring old real life.

'Are you sure you want to marry into this family?' Dad asks Jez. Outnumbered by eight breasts to none in the house, he's only partly joking.

'It's too late now, isn't it? Come on, Marley, we'd better go. I've got to be in the office early tomorrow.'

Marley hugs me again. 'This is going to be so much fun!'

But my head is spinning. How am I supposed to find the time to plan my sister's wedding when work already sucks sixty hours a week from my life?

Printed in Great Britain
by Amazon